Last Time Home

Susan Whitfield

ISBN: 978-0-9968187-2-8 (Trade paperback)
ISBN: 978-0-9968187-3-5 (eBook Edition)

Published in the United States of America

Smashwords Edition, License Notes

Published by Studebaker Press

Dedicated to my wonderful family, who love me in spite of my idiosyncrasies.

Last Time Home

Love is patient, love is kind. It does not envy, it does not boast, it is not proud. It does not dishonor others, it is not self-seeking, it is not easily angered, it keeps no record of wrongs. Love does not delight in evil but rejoices with the truth. It always protects, always trusts, always hopes, always perseveres.

1 Corinthians 13:4-7

1: CHRIS

Early March

After entering the one-mile square town limits of Atkinson, I drove my silver Toyota Highlander into the loose gravel driveway on Fourth Street beside the huge oak tree I'd climbed barefoot as a child. I smiled, thinking back to a time when Mama couldn't keep shoes on my feet because Daddy's lawn, a lush thick carpet of grass, kept me romping all over the property without shoes, only putting them on when scolded to do so.

As I pulled around to the back of the house, I noticed perhaps for the first time that the old house I'd grown up in had seen better days. The timeworn green shingled roof now sagged atop the vinyl-sided house—once white, but it now resembled an old gray mare with a sway back. At least the red brick foundation appeared to be in decent shape as far as I could tell. The pump house, although covered with ivy vines that looked like decaying bones, still stood outside the glassed-in back porch.

I parked by the broken sidewalk that encircled Mama's neglected rose garden, now over-run with leaves and small tree branches. I glanced at the old detached garage that offered protection for my Highlander from the ice that began to form on everything, but decided to leave it near the house so I could unload the grocery bags before my siblings arrived. As I got out, I looked over at the weary grape vines Daddy had pruned and been so proud of. I remembered picking luscious black grapes with him and running for the house if I encountered one of those hideous writing spiders. I shuddered at the thought and still hated spiders of any size. I twitched my nose, almost smelling the wonderful grape jelly Mama used to make but picking up instead the icy smell of bad weather on the way. I winced. I am the one who insisted that all five of us come this weekend and decide what to do about the contents of the house, now empty after Mama's death.

I turned my head toward the space that once grew a huge garden but now lay barren. I remembered Mama canning all that Daddy brought inside: butter beans by the bushel, garden peas, okra, crooked neck squash and big juicy tomatoes in several varieties. My mouth watered at the thought. Nothing could be finer than a loaf of fresh bread, strips of fried bacon, and Daddy's tomatoes. We ate BLTs almost daily in the summers.

Most of the trees near the house in my youth had come down long ago in one hurricane after another, the price for living about an hour from the Atlantic Ocean. I remembered Hurricane Hazel that had been so powerful it cross-hatched big pecan trees in the backyard as Mama snatched me away from the kitchen window. There were only two trees left now, one at the end of the driveway and one more near the end of the property line far away from any buildings. The sky looked ominous now, off to the west, and I feared the weather might take a nose-dive that made it difficult to do anything outside. However, there was plenty to deal with inside.

Shivering, I walked to the house and unlocked the creaking glass door with one key and then the wooden kitchen door with another, flipping on the lights since daylight quickly receded, even though it was early afternoon. When I had brought in the last of the groceries, maneuvering around Mama's elephant ear plant, still alive but in need of water, I set them on the kitchen table. I looked at the orange and yellow wallpaper Mama had loved so much just as the electricity flickered and went off, taking with it most of the day's light.

"No!" I spotted a flashlight and prayed that the batteries were still good. The light dimmed but offered me enough time to search for more light sources before total darkness set in. Because we had set the thermostat on 60 degrees in January, the house was comfortable but what warmth it held would escape quickly on one of the coldest afternoons we'd had all winter in eastern North Carolina. The temperature forecast promised a dip into record-breaking single digits overnight. I let out a cosmic sigh and hastened to find lights, throws and blankets to offer my four siblings when they arrived.

I studied the old fireplace as I walked by, wishing I'd bought a few bundles of wood at the Piggly-Wiggly in Burgaw on my way through. I shrugged, not sure building a fire in it would be safe anyway. I knew Mama hadn't used it in a long time, so I'd ask my brother, Pat, when he came. I grabbed my cell phone and texted him.

Lost power

Shortly he replied: *got wood?*

No

Pat texted back a frowny face followed by *Will circle back to town and get some.*

Thnx. Don't text and drive!

U started it

I smiled, but wondered if Pat even knew how to inspect the chimney or build a real fire. He had never been much of a hands-on guy but was smart when it came to numbers and banking.

I started to click on Eve's number but noticed my cell battery was down to one bar and I had no way to charge it. *Drat!* I really picked a fine time to get us all together to make decisions about the house and all its contents. I supposed I'd rushed a bit since Mama's death in January, but I needed closure and I felt like the others needed it too. I dreaded the ordeal most for Easter, who would no doubt be miserable and difficult in this weather. An accident in high school had left her in chronic pain that worsened as time went by. Grief, bad weather and tension would only add to the misery for all five of us.

Tension. I rubbed my stiff neck. Hallow and I had been somewhat closer as children but we'd left the nest first and the younger two girls had never really been close to us. Pat, the only male, was right in the middle. We had all come together to take care of our mother in her final days, but not all at the same time until the last day when awkwardness and sadness overpowered conversation.

I lifted the cedar chest lid and pulled out throws and blankets, wondering if the power would stay off all night. I peeked out the bedroom window, my concern growing as rain reached the trees, ground, grass and nearby road and seemed to freeze on contact. I prayed that my siblings would all arrive safely, unscathed by the nasty weather. Rifling through dressers and closets, I searched for more coverings just in case.

My cell binged weakly with another text from Pat:

Got food?

Eve bringing soup and bread,
I brought a few groceries,
I texted back.

K

I didn't know if the one remaining store in the tiny town carried groceries anymore and it wouldn't be open this late anyway, I thought as I glanced at my watch. The one café that had been the town hub a few years back had closed too.

My mother had died in January at eighty-nine, the funeral held on the coldest, dampest, darkest day I could remember. The burial at the Holliday family cemetery just outside of town was brief. People peered from under umbrellas and then scurried to their cars as the afternoon caved in with sleet, not much different from today. On that sad afternoon we siblings had simply locked the old house—still decorated with Christmas décor and a small artificial tree. We'd gone back to our daily lives in different parts of the state, only returning now to plow through all the material possessions left behind. I'd hoped for a sunny weekend, but Mother Nature had other plans. I should have known better.

Daddy died suddenly forty-five years ago, shattering my heart into a million tiny pieces. I'd never quite glued them back in place, no matter how hard I tried. After all, I'd known him longer than the others, and I'd been a daddy's girl, Mama being the strong disciplinarian and switching my young legs more times than I cared to remember. Whenever he did have to correct me, his gentle, disappointed voice and eyes made me want to bury myself under the floor and stay there. Disappointing Daddy wasn't something I ever wanted to do. I shivered now and reached for a soft dark teal throw to warm my back and shoulders while I waited, impatient and concerned for my brother and three sisters.

I, Christmas Noel Holliday Franklin, the oldest of five children born to John and Noel Holliday,

am now seventy-two years old. Relatives used to
tease Daddy that he wouldn't settle for any woman
unless her name made the Holliday name more
outstanding. As if by fate, he met Sarah Noel
Graham and married her in 1942. Much to my
Daddy's delight, each child arrived on or near a
holiday and was named after it or the month in
which the birth occurred. I started calling myself
Chris after being unmercifully teased by other
children in elementary school, along with some
of their parents. Even other relatives got into the
naming once in a while. I arrived on Christmas
afternoon, really stirring up the Holliday family
gathering when Mama's water broke while she
opened presents. I have been reminded of that
every year, even though it was not my fault.

Hallow, the next child, literally born on the
house's front steps on Halloween seventy years
ago, horrified trick-or-treaters. Still dramatic today,
she enjoys her wedding planning business. I, a
retired nurse, wished I could be invisible in my
sister's circles and watch her bring beauty and
precious memories to life for couples. Hallow's long
flowing red hair added to the drama, her mane
still a gorgeous color of red sunshine with just a
few hints of gray, like Mother's had been until age
seventy-five. Freckles dusted her nose and cheek
bones and I loved them. She didn't need makeup
but she wore it in an attempt to cover them. I
couldn't deny that she was a beautiful woman more

so than the rest of us girls. I had always thought she was the most confident as well. Hallow, ever flirtatious and vivacious—a hopeless romantic, had been married three times, but I wasn't sure if she still wore a wedding ring. As close as we'd been as children, our lives took us in different directions. I went to nursing school and began a career helping those who needed me. Even though I had hoped to revive the relationship after my sweet husband, Henry Franklin, died, it didn't happen. I suppose she stayed busy in Raleigh and probably thought I was stronger than I really was at that time. I ran my fingers through my long thick hair, now a silvery gold and soon to be all silver. I shook my head and let long pieces fan out around my shoulders, soft but not as shiny as Hallow's. Hallow and I shared our daddy's features.

John Patrick, the only male sibling, was tall and good-looking, his hair now salt-and-pepper, adding distinction to his sixty-eight years. He was a good mix of Daddy and Mama, born in March. I suppose my parents had to name him after Saint Patrick's Day. I had to wonder how many women banked at First National just to see the soft-spoken handsome man I knew as my brother. Even though married, Pat's wife, Phyllis, travelled the world for a large corporation and seldom attended family gatherings with him. She did manage to attend the funeral in January, though, much to our surprise. It wasn't that she wasn't a nice person; she was just usually not in the country to participate in anything.

Merry Eve Holliday Rockford, sixty-four, was born on New Year's Eve just before midnight. As a teacher, her fast-paced happy life ended when her husband, Matthew, died suddenly several years ago, leaving behind no will and a chaotic mess of an office at the real estate company. After months of getting nowhere, Patrick went to help her sort through and find papers necessary to prove beneficiary. It had been an ordeal for both of them and got the rest of the family checking for wills and other important paperwork. Mama had stayed with Eve and her daughter, Kirsten, for several months after the funeral. Eve hadn't remarried, and Kirsten, born when Eve was 39, joined the military after high school graduation. She now served in Germany. Eve looked more like Mama than the rest of us.

The youngest sister, Easter, was born in April sixty-two years ago. She'd been the family's fearless wild child in her youth, doing things the rest of us wouldn't dare, and covering much of her skin with tats that got no approval from parents or siblings. Her early lifestyle cost her dearly. She wrecked the car Daddy had bought her, going over one hundred miles an hour down a narrow tree-lined rural road, resulting in a lengthy hospital stay and injuries that caused more problems as the years went by. My beautiful sister never held a job and now lived on a monthly disability check with a sizable chip on her shoulder most of the time. She resembled Eve but her hair turned gray at an early age, and she embraced it.

I pushed open the door to the laundry room and the smell of detergent hit my nostrils. My eyes focused on Mama's big basket of yarn in sherbet colors, many knitting needles and crochet hooks in sizes big and small perched on a shelf over the washer and dryer. I smiled as I picked up a few skeins of angora. I had once used the warmest of these to knit Daddy a toboggan for Christmas. I preferred fuschia or turquoise personally, but settled for a two-tone gray, because, after all, I did want Daddy to wear it proudly. Each knit and perl was done with the love of a little girl who worshipped him. Love spun around each stitch. Looking back at the washer and dryer, I decided they could be sold with the house. I giggled as I thought about the time Mama had the bright idea to wash the mustard greens in the washing machine because they were full of dirt from the garden. The greens, of course, tore all to pieces and made a horrible mess for Daddy to clean up. He was steaming mad but didn't blow his stack. I loved that sweet man and still missed him so much. I wiped a tear away and closed the door when I heard the driveway gravel crunch under the weight of a vehicle.

2: EVE

I'd tried to tell Chris, my eldest sister, that the meteorologists predicted wintry precipitation, but *her* favorite weather man said all the bad stuff would stay on the western side of Interstate 95 and I had nothing to worry about. So as disgruntled as I was, I packed a few clothes and threw the bag into my old Acadia, stopping to gas up before traveling from Rocky Mount near the Virginia state line to my childhood home in Atkinson in southwestern Pender County.

I admit I was unhappy about more than the weather. I felt like it was too soon to go into Mama's house and take every single thing she'd ever owned out of it and divide it between the five of us children. Chris even wanted to sell the old house! My feelings include dread too. My three sisters and I had not been close in years, if we genuinely ever were close. Life stepped in and we drifted apart, building different careers in different areas of North Carolina and marrying men who had nothing in common with each other.

As I drove, thoughts of my sweet Matt crept into my mind, adding to my melancholy. It's incredible how fast your life can change from gloriously happy to devastatingly sad. Turn around on a dime, so to speak. Here one day, gone the next.

I suddenly slammed on brakes as a doe ambled into my path, trying to miss her but not run off the road. Thankfully she quickly turned back and I stayed on the road, relieved no car was in the other lane. I stayed on high alert for more animals as I rode farther south into more wooded areas but my mind quickly returned to Matt. Even though it has been three years, the grief lingered as if it happened yesterday. I wasn't certain that I even went through all the so-called phases of grief either. I'd gotten hung up in anger and resentment that Matt had suddenly abandoned me. *Us.* We had a daughter. I didn't mean to leave Kirsten out. We had done everything together— everything! Except for our work which took us in different directions during the day. But our nights, weekends and holidays were spent doing things we loved together, whether it was dining out, going to a movie, sitting on the porch with a drink, or watching a ball game. Kirsten had entered the military right out of high school. Now I felt lost. Companionless. Hollow. Empty.

Mama's death hadn't helped matters, not that she could help it. While the others, especially Chris, wanted to clean out the house and sell it, I wasn't ready to deal with it. But, then, when would I be? I glanced over at the crockpot I'd brought that was much bigger than Mama's and the boxes of broccoli cheddar soup I'd picked up at a local deli, knowing it would need to be heated when I got to the old home place. I looked forward to a hot bowl in this weather and knew the others did too.

3

Eve arrived and honked her horn. Chris bundled up and went to help her with the crockpot.

"No lights?"

"No *nothing*, I'm afraid," Chris declared. "I hope this soup is still warm." Chris peered through the glass lid into the empty space.

"Oh, dear. It's still in the boxes, I'm afraid. Room temperature at best. Take the pot on into the house, and I'll grab the soup, bread, and my overnight bag," Eve suggested, handing the huge crockpot to Chris. Chris walked gingerly to the steps, up to the porch, and used her pinkie finger to pull back the storm door. When she got to the counter, she sat the giant crock down, contemplating the dilemma.

Eve made a hasty entrance in her brown fur-collared pea coat and brought the bread and soup to the counter. "Since I had to drive from Rocky Mount, I figured I'd be the last one here. Where are the rest of them?"

"Well, Pat was on the way and I texted him about the power, so he went back to find firewood. He'll be here directly."

"Oh, good. I hope he brings *lots* of wood."

"I suppose whatever he can find at the last minute will have to do."

"Yeah, right." Eve kept her coat buttoned up.

"Can you believe this weather?" Eve cocked her head at Chris. "I know. I know. I said it would be fine, but apparently Elton Clapp was wrong this time."

"It's March in North Carolina, Chris. What did you expect? Besides, who'd believe a man named Clapp?"

"I know," Chris answered with a sigh. "I'd figured on cold, sunshine, and good ole electricity. November and December were so mild that I guess we've run out of luck."

"We ran out of luck the day we buried Mama." Eve's head dropped.

Chris nodded. "That's for sure. I guess I should have called ya'll and rescheduled, but I figured we all deal with the cold anyhow. I didn't factor in an ice storm and power outage."

"You couldn't have known about the power until you got here, Chris. And we were all on our way by then, I suppose. Anyway, who knew it would get this bad? The weatherman predicted 'cold' but he certainly didn't mention black ice." She touched Chris's arm. "I'm sorry I didn't warm up this soup before I left home. So sorry," she added with gritted teeth.

"It's okay. We'll make do. Mother Nature didn't hear his forecast, apparently. I'm worried about the others. Especially Easter even though she has a shorter drive than the rest of us."

4: HALLOW

I'd never felt that Mama loved me the way my friends' mothers seemed to love them. I don't know why. I never quite figured it out. As I drove from Raleigh back to the old home place, I couldn't get that feeling out of my head. Maybe it was the dreary sunless day with the threat of sleet that had my head and heart in a sad place, and those thoughts niggled at me again. As I had looked at her body in the casket back in January, I didn't feel much. Just some woman in a nice satin-lined casket for whom I was *supposed* to have feelings. But I never shed a tear. I didn't even feel the least bit sad. I sighed heavily now and tried to focus on the road and the traffic so that I didn't end up spinning out or getting involved in a nasty pileup.

I passed Garner and relaxed a bit once I got past Clayton, heading for the Smithfield exit where I would stop and relieve a full bladder. I dashed into the service station and grabbed a coffee on the way out in hopes that the caffeine would keep me alert. I still had a full hour's drive ahead of me on Interstate 40.

After two sips of hot coffee, the thoughts returned. There had always been a distance, a failure on her part to be affectionate. And I grew up needing affection. I remembered running in after school one day so excited to tell her I'd made the junior high cheerleading squad. I ran over to her at the kitchen sink and threw my arms around her waist.

"Get away from me! I don't have time for that mess!" she had called out in an ugly tone.

Even now at seventy, I could still remember the hurt as I fled out the door and decided if I ever had children, they would have no doubt how much I loved them.

I had always needed the affection, to hug and be hugged in return, to feel another body touch mine. Perhaps that's why I had been so promiscuous. Maybe that's why I sought love in all the wrong people.

Mama said I had been a flirt since I was three, madly "in love" with a teenaged boy who went to the same church. I learned to wink, and most folks thought it was cute. My flirtatious nature continued and my first real boyfriend gave me an Aurora Borealis necklace to let me know he liked me when we were in the sixth grade. Later when hormones kicked in, flirting with boys became practically a fulltime pastime. Still innocent, I had no idea where flirting could lead me. Stealing a kiss here or there was innocent enough until some boys stole a feel as well.

Feelings emerged that I'd never felt before. I wanted more. I had the urge to merge. Thinking back now as I passed through Duplin County, I was amazed that I hadn't completely ruined my life, gotten pregnant, or picked up some horrible disease. God had to have been protecting me. Didn't they say He protects babies and fools? I had undoubtedly been a *fool* for most of my life.

I could feel the tears coming as I grabbed my coffee cup and drained the last of its lukewarm goodness, looking skyward to thank God for looking after me even though I hadn't learned much in the years since. I was still a grade-A fool. Even at my age, I continued to do foolish things: trusting the wrong men, getting too close, and in the end getting scalded by all of them in one way or another.

But this *last* mistake took the cake. Not only did he take the *cake*, he also took nearly everything I owned. *Fool* isn't a strong enough word to describe me. I hadn't known him well enough to let him move into my gorgeous home, realizing too late that all along his purpose had been to take advantage of my stupidity at the first opportunity.

So here I was, heading home to get some of my dead mother's possessions and try to start over. My wedding planner business was hit and miss, and when I had a huge one, it paid handsomely. At other times I was just relieved I had my social security to fall back on. With all my belongings and expensive furniture gone and no wedding dates on the calendar, I feared I'd have to sell my dream home and start over in a tiny apartment like I had in my early twenties.

I gripped the steering wheel enough to have white knuckles. It wasn't just the awful weather that bothered me. Going home was always awkward, but now, even more so since Mama no longer lived there. Mama no longer lived anywhere. Mama no longer lived. A tear slid down my cheek for the first time since her death, and I wiped it away with my winter gloves, donned because my Acadia's heater had completely stopped working. Thank goodness I still had my long warm white coat. I'm surprised that poor excuse for a human being hadn't taken it and all my clothes too, as he had all pieces of high-end furniture, beautiful linens, vases, and many other of the prized possessions I'd treasured in my home.

I hit my gloved hands on the steering wheel. Duped! How could I have been so stupid, so

gullible? Hadn't I had enough experiences with
bad relationships to know one when I saw one?
Apparently not. I swallowed tears that were trying
to strangle me. My self-esteem took the biggest
hit of my life. After three failed marriages I'd
allowed my heart to over-ride my head once again.
And he had taken everything. The furniture wasn't
even the worst of it. I had allowed Tricky Dicky
to move in, and he had obviously found enough
financial reports and bank statements—that I'd
been trusting and careless enough to leave lying
around—to ruin me. My self-esteem was non-
existent at this point, and anger and humiliation
had taken the place of the confidence I once had.

My three sisters and I weren't close anymore.
If we had ever been. Chris and I had been closest
when we were still living at home, sharing bunk
beds and sometimes secrets although she was Miss
Goody Two Shoes to my flirtatious Jezebel. Chris
had married well; Henry Franklin was not only a
cutie but smart too. I married. For seven miserable
months. The other two sisters had been
somewhat closer and shared bunk beds, too, in
the same room with us until Chris and I graduated
and married. Our one brother, Pat, tried his best
to avoid all four of us, spending many nights with
friends in the neighborhood. I think he still avoids
us as much as possible to this day.

At any rate, I dreaded going to the old home
place to settle the estate "fairly." While I needed

pretty much everything in the house, I wouldn't get it. And I certainly had no intention of telling any of them that I'd been duped.

5

Chris and Eve heard a noise and turned toward the door as Hallow bolted into the house, shivering in a white furry coat pulled up under her chin.

"I'm frozen! My car's heater quit on the other side of I-95, and I'm looking forward to a warm fire . . . or at least furnace heat?" She bundled her coat and wrung her hands. "What gives?" She stared at her sisters.

"Power went out," they announced simultaneously.

"You've got to be kidding me."

"Sorry to disappoint, sis," Chris said, rushing to hug her, "no power and no wood for a fire. Pat went back to look for some." Hallow's age-defying face contorted.

"Isn't it an oil furnace?" She pointed a gloved finger at the metal monstrosity that took up too much room in the dining room corner.

"Yeah, but it takes an electrical spark to start it," Chris explained.

"Come snuggle with us until Pat gets here and builds a fire," Eve offered with outstretched arms.

Hallow stepped toward her sisters and they all cuddled.

6: PAT

I had taken the afternoon off to get to the old home place about the same time as my four sisters. I filled a travel mug with coffee—high test—and locked up the house. Even though the sky looked dark to the west, it was pleasant enough on the coast for a cold winter's day to drive to Atkinson and go through the house with my sisters. However, I wasn't looking forward to the bickering that would, no doubt, begin as soon as two of them wanted the same thing. Not that a single thing in the house had value. Heck, the house itself was dilapidated and wouldn't fetch much in the real estate market. Too far from most people's jobs, shopping centers, restaurants, and entertainment.

Chris would be in charge as usual. She was older and Executor of the Estate. I didn't envy her one bit, and I was relieved, as the only male, that the responsibility was not mine. My sisters were a force to be reckoned with. I sipped my coffee. With the roads getting more treacherous by the mile, I wondered how the others were faring. Especially Easter. I figured as much trouble as she'd had at Mama's funeral just getting out to the grave, I'd need to help her in this weather.

Now I was running behind because I turned around and came back into town to find some firewood. That turned out to be a challenge because most people had planned ahead, I supposed, and already bought up most of it. I traveled all the way across Wilmington to Monkey Junction and spotted a pile at a grocery store. I bought what was left even though it was a stiff price to pay, in my opinion. Once I loaded it, I headed west again.

7

The three sisters were still hugging for warmth when their brother pulled up.

Once he entered, the only brother in the Holliday brood wrapped his scarf tighter around his neck and threw out his arms.

"Hey," we all said in unison, kissing him and scrunching him into the huddle.

"Did you find wood?"

"Some," Pat reported, "I'm not sure it'll last all night, but it should be enough to take the chill off until bed time. By the way, Chris, what are the sleeping arrangements? I shoved my air bed into the back, but I'm not sure I can pump it without power."

"We have two beds, both regular sizes, so we girls will be fine. That leather couch doesn't open into a bed, but we can put sheets and blankets on it for you."

He nodded, looking around the room. "Where's Easter?"

"We haven't seen her, and I'm worried," Chris said.

"As well you should be," Pat said. "The roads are a slippery mess. I'd better go ride down highway 53 and make sure she hasn't gone off the road somewhere."

"Let's give her a few more minutes. You know she's always late anyway," Hallow expounded. "Hopefully, she's taking it slow and steady."

"Easter? We can only hope," Eve added.

"I'll bring the wood inside so it doesn't get wet and iced over. I bought a lighter too. Maybe I can get a fire started in that old thing," he said, looking at the old fireplace. "Got any old papers around here?"

"I want you to inspect it first to make sure it's safe. There's no telling when it was last used," Chris said.

"Inspect it? How am I supposed to do that?"

Chris shrugged her shoulders.

"I tried to get Mama to buy gas logs years ago, remember?" Eve asked. "But instead she bought a kerosene heater."

"I remember that thing. It scared me, but Mama loved it, and it did a good job keeping her warm as long as she stayed close to it," Pat replied.

"I wonder where it is?" He scratched his salt and pepper head, looking around.

"Probably out in the old shed," Chris said.

"I'll look for it after I bring the wood in. We may need everything we can find. Are there plenty of blankets here, Chris?"

"Yes, I don't think we'll lack for linens."

"I think we need to find Easter first," Hallow said. "Do you have plenty of gas, Pat?"

"Yes, I filled up when I went back into Wilmington for wood."

"Is your cell phone charged?"

"I have fifty percent and a charger in the truck. I'll charge mine again while I look for our sister. It should get us through the night, and we can all charge up tomorrow," Pat said

"I hope the power will be back on tomorrow."

"*Tomorrow*? What about *tonight*? We could freeze to death."

"We won't freeze, Eve. Plenty of blankets, and we can snug up close together if we have to and use our body heat."

"Or go to our cars and turn the heat on for a while."

"Yeah, I suppose we could do that, but I don't want to burn up all my gas."

"Be careful, Pat," Eve and Hallow said in unison as Pat finally made it out the door to search for their baby sister just as headlights swung into the yard and Easter's little VW bug eased up as close to the house as possible.

"Thank God!" Chris said, putting her hand over her heart.

"I'll get her," Pat called back.

8: EASTER

I got behind a bivouac coming out of Jacksonville, Marines from Camp LeJeune on the move. Many good-looking soldiers waved as I passed a few trucks loaded with Humvees and tanks, slipping in between them as traffic approached. I waved back with a smile. They didn't know I was damaged goods. Deep nasty scars covered both legs that had been badly mangled, and most of my left arm had deep puncture wounds from breaking glass. I never wore skirts or dresses, only long pants, even during the hottest days of summer. My right wrist had been so badly shattered that metal pins held it together and it still bothered me most of the time. My left hand was not in bad shape, all things considered, and my face had been spared.

When I passed the lead truck, I blew my Beetle's horn and sped up, then realized enough black ice had formed on the highway to ditch me, so I slowed back down. Not the best day for driving. Not the best day for going through the house and Mama's personal stuff. But when would be a good day?

I lived a fairly solitary life, not by choice. Well, maybe it *was* by a choice I made in high school, but anger simmered just below the surface, never dissipating after all these years. Anger at *myself*, nobody else. It had all been me. My choice. I didn't mean to take my wrath out on others. It just happened. I'd popped a gasket. Rant. Melt-down.

I told myself that I would behave this weekend and not be negative, although Chris sure did pick a fine weekend to "settle things" and "have closure." She'd always been the boss of us. First, as Mama and Daddy's drill sergeant and then later just because she was older. Not sure about the "wiser" part, though. I smirked. Chris had a sweet disposition and a good heart, but that bossiness was hard to swallow. She did have a nursing degree, though, and I had never used my art degree in any shape or form. I'd chosen that direction because I could sit at an easel and paint without having to move around too much, happy that I had inherited my mother's artistic talent.

Chris. I supposed it was tough being the oldest of five children but being the youngest was no picnic either—worse in my opinion. I was expected to follow in the footsteps of the four older ones and be all they were. Make the outstanding grades Chris and Pat made. I wasn't dumb; I just didn't give a happy flip flop. I made Cs and Ds and nearly failed Algebra. I sat in the back of the classroom with the boys and shot spitballs off Mr. Moore's bald head. My aim was spot-on, and my thumps forceful. I giggled even now just thinking about it. That man had no idea a girl was doing it, and the boys didn't rat me out. But my senior year was fraught with pain and the agony of rehab. Hallow was a drop-dead gorgeous redhead with flawless peaches and cream complexion—rare in our family. She'd made decent grades and cheered in high school, boys lining up to date her. Eve, the closest to my age, was meek and mild to my loud and wild, and she was possibly the most studious of all of us. I'd really never hit it off with her or my other sisters. I guess I was considered the Black Sheep of the family. I winced at the thought.

When I was sixteen, Daddy got me an old clunker sedan I called a tank even though what I *really* wanted was a little MG convertible. He'd said "no" because money was tight and my safety concerned him. He'd told me I'd get killed in one of those tiny cars. And when I *did* wreck going over 100 miles per hour, I sustained life-threatening injuries that I would never get over. Yes, Daddy was right, of course. The MG would have tossed me out, and I would've eaten my last supper—black pavement.

I'd spent most of my last two years of high school in the hospital in traction and then learning to walk again. Once I recovered well enough to drive again—almost ten months of healing and therapy—I watched my speed and tried to act like I had good sense, most of my injuries to my legs, feet, and pride. Although my siblings had all eventually married, I hadn't. I barely dated. Who wanted to be shackled with damaged goods? I had to admit, though, that my family, wherever they were, came to visit me often in the hospital to keep my spirits up.

Now as I approached the city limits of the small town and turned on Fourth Street, I tried to get my feelings to a happier place as sleet stuck to the windshield. My legs hurt even though it had taken less than forty-five minutes from my house. Every muscle in my body cried out. I sighed deeply before trying to extricate myself from the cramped Beetle—that I thought I had to have because Daddy had one just like it when I was young—and put my feet on solid ground. At least I hoped it was solid and not black ice waiting to throw me off balance.

9

The three sisters braced themselves and waited for Easter. Pat struggled to get her across the icy drive, into the house and over to the La-Z-Boy recliner. Cold air rushed in behind them and dropped the house's temperature even more.

"I'll get your cane and walker," Pat told her before heading back out and closing the door.

"Get my clothes, too. I may have to put all of them on right now," she grumbled. Easter's three sisters surrounded her and warmed her shivering shoulders and legs, throwing a red-knit cable throw over her.

"Since it seems unlikely that the power will come back on during the night, let's search for more blankets and candles," Chris said. "Hopefully Mama kept extra batteries for the flashlights too.

This one little light isn't going to last much longer. I know there used to be a huge one around here somewhere, and it used D batteries."

"That was Daddy's big flashlight. It's old but heavy-duty and if we can find it and some batteries, that'll be great," Pat added, still in his coat.

"I gave her a couple of battery-operated candles for Christmas last year. Maybe we can find those," Hallow added. "And we need to settle our sleeping arrangements before it gets too dark to do that," she pointed out.

"Yeah, I'm going to do that right now," Easter said, fumbling her way out of the recliner and grabbing her cane.

"Remember that you'll have to sleep with one of us," Chris called after her youngest sister. She watched her sister's shoulders slump in disappointment.

"I have to pee," Easter announced and went into the one tiny bathroom that had been shared by Mama, Daddy, and five children.

"Don't flush!"

Pat headed for the backdoor. "I'm going to the barn with my cell phone's light. Hopefully I can find some useful items to help us get through the night."

By the time all the ladies used the bathroom, Pat returned with their father's huge flashlight and flipped it on, its light dim but working. "We may be able to find some fresher batteries in a drawer somewhere. Mama always kept plenty, just in case."

They each took a light source of some kind and scrambled in different directions on a mission to find more blankets and items that would come in handy if, indeed, the electricity stayed off the whole weekend. Sounds of drawers opening or closing, paper rattling, something falling to the floor, and a few other bumps filled the house before they reconvened in the living room. Pat had gone back outside for additional items.

"I found another flashlight by Mama's bed," Easter said proudly.

Pat fumbled through the backdoor with a kerosene heater. His sisters all smiled and nodded. "Don't get your hopes up. I doubt it has any fuel," he said.

Eve reached out her hand. "Here, I have some matches I found in the kitchen drawer. See if that baby will work." Pat took the matches but hesitated.

"Whoa! I'm going to check it over good before I light a match."

"Oh, yeah, good idea."

Hallow put a beautifully decorated candle on the table. "Mama never burned this one. It's still wrapped in dingy cellophane."

"I remember that. Somebody gave it to her for directing a wedding and she didn't want to mess up the wax flowers all over it," Chris said.

"Yeah, I remember it too," Eve added. "I think it was our cousin Kim's wedding and we all wore fuchsia dresses that Mama made."

"And Mama made herself a rose dress too. She sure could sew," Easter said, her voice cracking.

"And that was a long time ago," Hallow added. "The whole thing has yellowed."

"I didn't get the sewing gene," Chris said.

"None of us did, Chris. Especially me," Eve chimed in.

"There have to be more candles because people gave Mama so many at Christmas time and I doubt she ever lit most of them. Yellow or not, they should burn."

"Oh, while looking for flashlights I found a trunkful of quilts but they smell like cedar."

"I don't care as long as they warm me up," Easter replied. "I actually like the smell of cedar."

"You're weird," Eve teased her. Easter stuck out her tongue.

Hallow lit candles and moved a couple to the kitchen table without joining the conversation. Chris noticed age lines had formed around her beautiful sister's eyes. The eyes themselves sagged. Her color was pale and her usually-confident shoulders slumped. Her face wore an emotion Chris had never seen before. Something was definitely going on.

"Hallow, are you okay?"

Her face blanched. "I'm fine."

"Let's eat. I'm starving!" Pat called out. Chris decided now was not the time to ask more questions. They all agreed to eat and gathered around the table.

After they had bowls of lukewarm soup and most of a loaf of bread Eve had brought, they decided who would sleep where. Pat, of course, would get the couch or their daddy's old recliner, but the four sisters would have to share double beds. Chris thought maybe she and Hallow would share a bed and maybe she could find out what was eating her sister.

10

Chris's eyes popped open and she could see a hint of daylight. She tried to move her hair out of her eyes.

"Ow!" Hallow called out. "Don't pull my hair."

"Sorry, thought it was mine," Chris said, throwing the cover back and getting out of the lumpy bed. "I'm going to put on some coffee."

"The power's back on?"

"Oh, I forgot about that. Apparently it's not, because it's freezing in here." She bundled herself into a short bathrobe she'd found in the bathroom and tucked her long hair around her neck.

"Well, I'm staying in here where it's warm," Hallow whispered, rolling over to occupy the entire bed.

Chris peeked in the other bedroom at the humps of Eve and Easter buried under covers. At least they had found enough cover to keep them all warm. Pat had already pulled sheets and blankets from the couch and folded them neatly. He was in the kitchen.

"Morning."

He turned. "Good morning. No power, but at least the sun's coming up and it's supposed to get into the forties. That should warm up the house a bit." Chris hugged him and looked around.

"I'm not sure what we can do as far as breakfast."

"Oh, I went out to the garage and brought Daddy's rusty old grill up here and lit a fire in it to burn off the rust and dust. If I can find some foil, I'll put on a coffee pot and whatever else we can find. I'm glad I picked up a bag of charcoal."

"Country folks can survive, huh?"

"I sure hope so," he said, winking at her. "I looked in the fridge and found some milk and butter, though. It stayed fairly cold since we kept the door shut."

"I brought them and threw out the outdated stuff in there. I know we have more bread and some cereal, so maybe we can at least have breakfast. I should have picked up some eggs, too, but I never thought of it." Chris pulled open a cabinet and searched. "Ah, here's some jelly, and it's not out-of-date." She handed him a roll of tin foil.

"Good. I'll wrap the grill," Pat said.

"Good man."

Chris heard shuffling feet and turned to smile at Eve and Hallow, both yawning. "Good morning, gals."

"What's good about it," Eve snapped.

"Well, we made it through the night and the sun's out, and we're in the process of making some breakfast for you," Chris said with a positive tone.

"We have power?"

"No, but I brought some groceries. Pat picked up some charcoal, so we *can* survive."

Eve dropped into a chair, pouting. "I didn't sleep a bit. Easter snored with her mouth open all night long. I'm ready to go home." She grumbled something more under her breath.

"If the power doesn't come back on, I guess we should *all* go home this afternoon before dark and try another weekend. At least let's decide how we want to divide all the personal property so that it's fair to all of us," Chris said.

"I agree with that," Hallow added.

"What if we want the same things?" Eve asked.

"That's what we need to work out. How we will handle that so nobody leaves with hurt feelings."

Easter's cane made a noise as she worked her way into the room. "What about hurt feelings?"

Pat came to the door and announced that he had put the coffee on. They all clapped.

"Don't let me forget to check that chest freezer out in the shed. If it warms up any, that food will start to thaw."

"Ain't no food going to thaw in *this* weather," Easter said with an ugly tone.

"Well, the sun's out and warming up fast, so I'd better check it. If the power stays off, we'd better take anything that's good home with us."

The sisters busied themselves making jelly sandwiches to have with their coffee.

"I've been thinking about how to divide things up," Chris said after the five had sat down at the dining room table with their make-shift breakfast. "I don't want us to end up like some families do, not speaking to each other again over some *thing.*"

They all nodded agreement.

Pat put his hand out on the table toward them. "How about numbering everything with our personal number? Then whoever wants it can fight it out."

"That's what I want to avoid. No fighting," Chris added.

"I didn't mean—"

"I know you didn't."

"We could use Post-it notes and assign each a number to put on things. If nobody else puts a sticker on it, it belongs to that person," Eve said. "I may have some in my car in enough colors for all of us."

"We could at least start out that way, I suppose and see how it goes," Hallow said.

"Are we seriously going to put a number on everything in this house? That could take months!" They all looked over at Easter, who'd made a valid point.

"Like things together," Eve suggested.

"I don't know about that now," Hallow said. "Who wants all of the same things?"

"But I think we should all have one of Mama's pots and one of her blankets, her handmade quilts, and so on," Eve suggested. "I think there are plenty for all five of us to have at least one or two."

"True, we should each get a fair share of dishes, pots and pans, linens, and other stuff." Pat ran his fingers through his thick hair again. "I just don't know how."

"Well, let's just pull stuff out from one room at a time, even closets and cabinets. Set it all on this table and decide on that. Then we could load our stuff into our vehicles and move on from there," Eve suggested. "Wouldn't that work?"

"There are probably plenty of things that can go right in the trash, too," Chris pointed out.

"Like what?" Eve had sat up at attention, her eyes bugged.

"Like ragged wash cloths and towels, stained kitchen towels and oven mitts, clothing with holes or out-of-date stuff. I saw some sheets that are thread-bare and not worth hauling home."

"That's a matter of opinion," Eve countered. They quieted and looked at her.

Pat stood with frustration written all over his face. "Okay, we're getting nowhere fast, and it's almost eleven o'clock. I'm going to charge my cell in the truck and check in with Phyllis." His steps were heavy as he walked away from them.

"Let's try the sticky notes and numbers and see how it goes, Eve. But we *do* need a few rules," Chris said.

"And I'm sure you're going to tell us *your* rules," Easter said with an ugly face.

"Would you like to make the rules, Easter?"

"Not really, but why are you always the one telling us what we can and can't do?"

"Easter, quit acting like a spoiled child. Chris is the oldest, and we *do* need some kind of rules," Hallow said. Easter harrumphed and looked away. "Go ahead, Chris."

"Well, I'm not trying to be bossy, but we need to agree on a few things. Since I'm the oldest, I am the executor of the estate. Mama did that and made it *clear*, Easter. I'd be happy not to be in this position. Everything, including the house and property, are to be divided fairly and equally. With *all* of this," she waved her arms around the piles," we need to agree to take turns, to not remove things without everyone's permission and knowledge, and to agree to get along so that we don't take the entire year trying to do this. Can't we just get along enough to get this done? If we can't even agree on how to start, we'll never accomplish anything. I'm sure Mama is looking down on us right now, wishing she could switch our legs!" Chris realized her voice grew louder with an ugly edge and she stopped talking.

"I'll go get those sticky notes and tell Pat we're ready to start," Eve said after a few seconds of silence.

"Thanks," Chris whispered.

"And I'm going to pee while that's happening," Hallow announced, rising from her seat.

Chris leaned toward Easter. "I'm sorry you think I'm bossy. I'll be glad to let you take charge if you want to."

Easter shrugged and shook her head.

"Why are you so angry, Easter?"

"You have no idea."

"No, I don't. That's why I'm asking. Have I done something to offend you, to cause this hostile attitude?" Chris could tell her voice had gotten loud again.

Easter sighed deeply. "It's not *you*." She waved her hands over her body. "Look at me. I can't do jack, and I hurt most of the time while my used-to-be friends are out having a life."

Chris bit her lip and sat down close enough to her youngest sister to touch her knee. "I know that I have no idea how it feels to be in your situation, but—"

"Don't even say it, Chris!"

"Say what?"

"That Mama and Daddy warned me about being a dare devil and this is what I deserve."

"Honey, no! That's not what I was gonna say at all."

"Well, what then?"

"Perhaps we should postpone this conversation until you're not so hostile."

"I'm nearly *always* hostile," Easter admitted, lowering her voice and head.

"Then maybe you need some help."

"A shrink?"

"No!" Chris got up and slapped her hips in frustration. "No, Easter."

"Well, just so you know, I've seen several, and they're just after my money," Easter confessed.

Chris blinked at that confession. "I think this is too tough to do alone, and you're looking in all the wrong places, baby girl," Chris said, perching on the side of her sister's chair.

"You haven't called me that since we were kids." Chris smiled. "Where should I be looking then?"

"Would you be receptive to going with me to church?" Easter blinked. "You know," Chris continued, "like we did when we lived in this old house and Mama sang in the choir, and Daddy was a deacon."

"You're back in church?"

"Yes, Henry and I used to go on Sundays but after he died, I just couldn't pull myself together until I went back, you know? I was going through the motions but kinda floating around with my head not focused at all. I don't know how I got through the days. They're all a blur, but when I picked myself up, pulled out a Sunday outfit, and made up my mind to go, rain, sleet, or snow, I began to get better, come out of the fog." She paused to look at Easter, who only blinked again. "We have a wonderful church, Easter. Some of those people have been through unimaginable horrors—stage four cancer, losing a child, and so much more, and their faith got them through all of it. It's amazing how many miracles are in our one church. Even our pastor has a past, but God touched him and all the rest, and it's the best place in the world to go for acceptance and peace. They comforted me in so many ways. You need to forgive yourself, too, Easter."

"Wow, you've really bought into it."

"Like never before. I've always believed in God but now I have a stronger, more powerful sense of His presence with me at all times. I'm born again. It's the most wonderful feeling you can imagine!"

"And that's how you stay calm, cool, and collected?"

"Well, it helps. I still get out of whack sometimes. You know, sad or disgruntled over some silly mess, but God pulls me back in, and I return to peace."

"I've never seen this passion in you," Easter said, wobbling up and getting her walker. "Please excuse me. I gotta use the bathroom. Sorry."

The moment had passed, but Chris hoped she'd planted a seed. She realized the year-and-a-half their homebound mother was ill, it had been *her* idea for them to take turns instead of all of them coming at once. When the house was full of noise, her mother was agitated and annoyed. It seemed better to break the care into five parts, but it hadn't brought the brood closer together. That much was certain.

Shortly the five of them all convened again to try the sticky notes.

Eve passed them. "Okay, I'm assigning colors and I don't want any lip," she announced. "Easter, you are blue, Pat, you get lavender—"

"What is lavender?" They all giggled.

"*I'll* take lavender and he can have blue," Easter said, swapping with her brother.

"Okay, moving on then, Hallow is orange, Chris is white and I'm yellow."

They each picked up their packs of stickers.

"Why don't we look over all of this that's already out and stick our color on things we want? Everything else can go to the side for later," Chris offered.

"What about several colors on one item?"

"Then we can draw straws or something," Hallow said.

"I don't have any luck with drawing straws. I don't think that's fair," Easter said emphatically.

Pat touched her hand, "We have to start somewhere, Easter. Let's see how it goes."

The siblings took their colors and shopped the table and counters, marking pots, pans, utensils, cookie sheets, dishes, coffee mugs, and glassware. Eve ran out of notes quickly.

"My goodness, Eve! You can't have *everything!*" Easter shouted at her sister.

"I didn't put a note on *everything*. You're free to put a color on anything that interests you," Eve added in an ugly tone.

Pat leaned toward Chris and whispered, "I'm already irritated."

Chris nodded. "Yep, the laugher didn't last long."

Hallow hadn't said much but studied items and put an orange sticker on quite a few. Chris put a sticker on one pot and the everyday dish stack, but she knew she could live without either if it became a problem. Pat hadn't used any of his colors. It seemed that Eve, Easter, and Hallow would have a heated competition for most of the wares.

When the dust settled only a few items remained without at least one sticker. Pat walked over to the old ugly bent cookie sheet that looked as if it had been run over by a truck. "If nobody else wants this baby, I'll take it."

"Why on earth?" came the question in unison.

"Sentimental value," he said, taking the ugly pan in his hand. "I guess Mama used this to bake sweet potatoes because they always oozed out and it had to be scrubbed. And the peanut brittle hardened on it during the winter, and she could just snap the pan and release the brittle. I've never had any as good as she could make."

The four sisters smiled and nodded.

"Boy, would I love some of her brittle right now," Hallow said, licking her lips.

"Okay," Chris clapped her hands. "Let's get all this stuff with only our color into our vehicles. Then we can figure out how to divvy the rest that has more than one color on it.

As they gathered things to carry out, the electricity hummed, and a lamp came on.

"Yippee! Hopefully it'll stay on and warm up so we can keep at it," Hallow said.

Eve found a box of Dominoes, and they decided to each draw one for each item they wanted, and whoever had the highest number got the item. It seemed to work well for a while.

A pile of magazines from 1983 through 2000 had no notes. "Can we all agree to trash these?"

"Wait, Chris. Couldn't some retirement homes maybe use them?"

"I doubt it, Hallow. I mean these are extremely old." Chris looked around and everyone nodded except Eve. "Okay. We're trashing them, right?"

"I…um," Eve struggled, "um, okay."

"Right." Pat picked up the wobbly pile and stuffed them into a trash bag Easter held out.

"I got all these old medical bills and junk mail out of Mama's top drawer. Some of them are so old they can't possibly be needed at this point," Pat pointed out. "Besides, all the outstanding bills, including the funeral, have been paid. I'll burn these."

"What are we going to do with Mama's old Buick Regal?"

"I think it might still be in good shape, although it won't crank. Probably needs a new battery, cables, and oil change, and it'll run just fine," Pat said. "Anybody want it?" No one said anything. "Okay, I'll see what I can get for it and we'll all split the money. I can tell you it won't be enough to get excited about."

Daddy's old railroad depot clock was next, and it had five notes on it. The 30-day clock had to be wound up, had a brass pendulum and still worked just fine. The last documented repair was in 1935. It ticked and tocked but didn't bing, bong, or chime. It was also one of the few things that still connected them to their father. They passed over it because it would, no doubt cause the calm they were in at the moment to fade fast.

"What about this table," Hallow asked. "I could use it if nobody else wants it." She stuck a post-it on it.

"The kitchen table and chairs need to go too," Easter added. "I just don't have room for any big stuff in my apartment."

"There's a picnic table outside that seems to be in pretty good shape. Needs sanding, though," Pat said.

"Well," Chris said, "over here are a gazillion baskets of Mama's. Just post what you want. I want one but it doesn't matter which."

"Yeah, I feel the same way," Pat replied. Eve, Hallow, and Easter posted several notes on each.

Back in the kitchen they passed by all the canned goods that Chris had pulled from all the cabinets. "Throw expired ones in that big basket lined with a yard bag, and Pat can haul them off too."

"Oh gosh, I remember Mama and her beans," Hallow said, picking up a can of navy beans. "She'd say, 'if I eat all these beans, I'll be singing a tune.'"

They all laughed and the task before them seemed easier.

❋ ❋ ❋

Tension just beneath the surface became more noticeable to all of them the next morning. Was it the weather or the fact that all five of them were under one small roof with no way out?

As the day warmed and sunlight lit up memories through the house, the five siblings pulled items out of the top kitchen cabinets until no room remained on the counters or the large table for anything else.

Chris pulled out the kitchen drawer and set it on the counter, rifled through to sort items by function, and stopped when she picked up the tongs.

"Hey, Pat, do you remember when Daddy sent you into the kitchen to get Mama's 'thongs'?"

Pat burst into laughter. "Yeah, I sure do," he snorted. "I nearly peed my pants. We all ended up having a good laugh over that one."

Hallow spewed iced tea, trying to cup her hands to stop the flow to the floor. "That was hilarious. Daddy could come up with some good ones, couldn't he?"

"Yeah, and he was serious too." Pat stopped laughing. "I sure do miss that sweet man." All the girls nodded and stayed quiet for a moment.

Later in the day they went through the small china cabinet, pulling everything else out onto the table. Hallow and Eve handed fragile glass items to Easter, who organized them on the table. Chris pulled out the large wide drawer at the bottom, and handed off placemats in sets of eight for Eve to pass to Easter. Some were plastic or vinyl to use with soup, spaghetti and other messy foods. Some were dressier and saved for company or birthdays. The ones on the bottom were hand-crocheted and stiffly starched.

"I remember when Mama did these. She was so talented. If you tried to buy these nowadays, they'd be at least twenty dollars apiece."

"At least," Hallow figured.

Chris reached for a pile of beautiful tablecloths, most of them showing their mother's sewing skills. One beige tablecloth had cutwork at each corner in thread a little darker to show it. Chris looked at the stitches closely, amazed at how perfect each one was. She handed it off and reached for a white one with red poinsettias cross-stitched on it. Passing it off, she dug deeper into the drawer and pulled out a green cloth and handed it to Eve. There were enough crocheted doilies for each of them to have at least two. They'd been used under bowls and lamps to keep from scratching the furniture.

11: CHRIS

Home sweet home. Back in Morehead City after the nasty weekend with my siblings, I sighed with relief. Nasty on all counts. The weather was horrendous. The lack of electricity just put the icing on the cake. Misery times five. And I got blamed for picking this particular time, of course.

Why, I kept asking myself, did it have to be so hard for five adult siblings to get along? Were other families like ours? I had to think not. Even though the weekend ended on a decent note, there had been so much tension, mistrust, and conflict that I developed a terrible headache. Sure, we could disagree, but there seemed to be no willingness to agree on much of anything. Lack of respect seemed evident among us. I felt a rogue tear slide down my cheek and roughly rubbed it away.

I poured myself a glass of wine and picked up a thick yellow blanket from the sofa and walked to the French doors that led to the deck. Even though the sea breeze was crisp, I sat in my rocker and looked out across my little piece of land attached to the Atlantic Ocean, slowly inhaling briny air. My hands shook even though I should have had time to calm down on the two-hour ride. Sometimes I just wanted to slap Easter to China! But she wasn't the only one out of sorts. All five of us had seemed on edge. Eve and Hallow nearly came to blows over several insignificant items. It just didn't make any sense to me. I was relieved to be out of it for a while.

Home. My beautiful home, my happy place, where I could have much-needed solitude. The house on the ocean was built ten years after our marriage. Henry had designed and insisted on building it to my specifications. As a contractor, he did most of the work himself while I worked as a nurse at the small local hospital in Beaufort. We lived in a duplex apartment until it was finished. The first level of the house featured parking for three vehicles—my SUV and his two trucks. Inside the first-floor entryway, stairs led up to the other two levels. A built-in closet elevator stood next to them. I had argued against such a luxury but was glad we had it when Henry became sick.

Cancer left him in a weakened state, and without it, we would have had to sell the house and move into a patio home for easy access. This level also included a small mud room with sink and toilet.

The second level contained three bedrooms in case family or friends visited, and two full baths and an office and a small den. None of this floor had been used much, but we did enjoy the office. The third level included a living room, kitchen, dining area, and the master suite. The suite had his and hers walk-in closets as well as a walk-in shower. That had been another great decision since it allowed me to give Henry my best efforts right up until the end of his life, only calling the EMS for help the night he started convulsing. He hadn't made it to the hospital.

A gust of cold winter air encircled me and I shivered and gulped my wine, went inside to shower, and tuck sad memories away. I peeked through the blinds at the full moon, spotlighting the waves near the shoreline. I felt a smile ease across my face, thinking about how Henry had picked such a beautiful property on which to build our dream house and knew that tomorrow would be a new and more pleasant day.

I rose early, bundled up and went for a walk along the shore because a mild breeze and the sun brought warmth to the winter's day. My night had been fitful with much twisting and turning and intermittent snatches of arguments with disagreeable people that left me ill as an agitated snake. I walked two miles and turned around to head back as the wind shifted and came straight out of the north. I hurried my steps, relieved to duck into the entry and head up to the kitchen. A cup of hot chocolate would be my first order of business. I inserted a pod into the Keurig and prayed that God would bless me with a wonderful day and insightfulness in dealing with my family and all the estate that I as Executor must handle.

I flipped open a plantation shutter and smiled at the blue ocean, the sun beams dancing on its surface like diamonds. This view always calmed me. A shrimp boat trawled off in the distance and two jet skiers raced past the window. Following in their wake were six pelicans undulating just above the waves. My smile broadened.

My family. We had been a fairly close family during most of my early childhood. Hallow, Pat, and I had climbed trees, shot B-B guns, raced bikes down Fourth Street, and we girls loved to roller-skate down Highway 53 when traffic was elsewhere. Eve and Easter were too young to join in our kind of fun, so we watched from the tree as they hopscotched and hula-hooped instead. But once I graduated, it seemed a switch flipped and nothing was ever the same with them or to be honest, Mama and Daddy. I felt like an alien. I guess that's kind of how Pat had *always* felt. Like he didn't fit in with all the girls. And he to this day still seemed uncomfortable in his own skin and life, at least around his family.

My thoughts drifted back to Mama. She'd had a full life, married a wonderful man, and gave him five children. She could sketch a beautiful dress in a store window, go to a fabric store and buy materials and make an outfit for pennies on the dollar. She saved an inordinate amount of money over the years until we girls begged for store-bought clothes, not realizing how special our handmade garments were. Daddy had been so proud of her when she decided to go to business school, quickly landing the position of Secretary of the School of Education at Wilmington College as soon as she graduated.

At the age of 60 she'd bought art supplies and an easel to begin painting oils, mostly landscapes, to fill the void left by Daddy's death. All of us were grown and out of the house so the living room became her art gallery. She started The L Club—Live Longer and Love It—planning programs and asking ladies to bring covered dishes for lunch. The Atkinson community signed up. Retired single men got into the act, probably for the good food and the possibility of winking at a few of the widowed ladies in the group. Mama sang in the church choir for thirty years. She often sang solos in her angelic soprano and sang in nearly every wedding ceremony in town. She also taught a Sunday School class for about forty years.

Thinking back now, I realized just how talented Mama had been. But Daddy's sudden death had changed her. She became much more opinionated and vocal, often embarrassing us adult children in front of others. It dawned on me that maybe she had always had that underlying disposition, and Daddy had been able to keep her under control with his soft sweet demeanor. She then became more and more challenging to be around, and I sometimes found an excuse not to go home because I didn't feel strong enough to deal with her. I felt guilty about that, but I figured I had to do what was best for me. I was relieved that the stroke took her in January without months or years of being an invalid. That wouldn't have been easy on her or the rest of us. We would have had our hands full dealing with her mood swings and demands. My thoughts floated away as I looked back at the Atlantic Ocean. I let out a loud sigh and set about straightening the house before I drove to my dental appointment.

12

Late March

Pollen blew in on a chilling wind as daffodils and azalea buds emerged just in time for light snow and cold temperatures to burn them overnight. Winter's transition into spring in North Carolina was volatile to say the least. Chris wrapped her new wool tunic around her as tight as possible and crushed on a hat even though she didn't like wearing one. Staying well was more important right now.

She had convinced her siblings to go back to the old home place on the last weekend in March, and she prayed that the electricity would stay on and the five of them could make tremendous progress in emptying the house. She had checked the weather forecast, in the high fifties or low sixties with only a slight chance of rain all weekend. She had also realized that their father's birthday was that Sunday, the 25th, so she would stop at a deli in Burgaw and pick up a cake or maybe a lemon pie—her daddy's favorite—and a few other items to celebrate his life along with the large roast she'd cooked. She wiped a tear and decided what to pack, since she had persuaded the others that they must attend church on that special Sunday morning. In addition to her jeans and sweatshirts, she pulled out a royal blue dress and some low heels to attend the Southern Baptist church where they'd gone every Sunday as children.

Chris and Pat were already in the old house when they heard the other three coming in noisily.

"I'm almost positive I didn't put a slip in my bag," Eve said.

"A *slip*? Who wears a slip anymore?" Easter chortled.

"I do!" Hallow admitted. "Mama always told us not to let the sun show anything between our legs."

"Well, a slip won't fix *that*," Easter erupted in a guffaw, and Eve grinned but kept her mouth shut.

"*Hey!* Be nice," Chris called out to them with an ugly tone as Hallow's face reddened.

"I see the boss is here first, as usual," Easter said, giving Chris the evil eye.

"Nice to see you too, Easter." Chris turned away from them.

"Oh, for Pete's sake! Knock it off! Y'all are too old to act like a bunch of toddlers!" Pat yelled loud enough to bounce a dish off the side table near him.

CRASH!

Startled by the noise, they all froze and opted for an uncomfortable silence. Eve headed to the kitchen and came back with a broom and dust pan, not saying a word or looking at any of them. Pat ran his hands through his hair. "*I* should clean that up."

"I've got it," Eve said in a calm voice with a slight smile.

Chris admired the way she held herself together all the time, even now. She remembered that dish she'd bought for their mother to keep beside her reading chair to hold an afternoon or night snack. This one was gold with a red bird, and there was another one somewhere in blue. Chris stayed silent for a while, studying her siblings. Hurt attached itself to each of them in different ways, she figured, from all-encompassing grief to losing some small token that held special memories. Chris let out a loud sigh and all heads turned in her direction, causing her to blush and leave the room.

"I didn't mean to start anything with my slip issue," Eve said.

"You'll be fine without a slip. And I'll leave mine off too. In fact, I might wear pants like Easter's going to do," Hallow added with a softer voice.

Pat gathered the three sisters closer to him. "Look, Chris is a little sad, okay? Sunday would have been Daddy's birthday. Let's try to be respectful of each other *for a change*. Is that too much to ask?" They shook their heads and went off in different directions to put away their things and calm down.

Pat found Chris in their mother's bedroom, pulling things out of drawers and placing them on the bed.

"Are you crying?"

Chris jumped, startled by her brother's presence behind her. "Oh! I didn't hear you come in." She brushed tears from her eyes and managed a smile.

"So?" Pat looked her dead in the eyes.

"I just hate for everything to be so difficult. I suppose once all this is settled, we go back to being distant. All of us, Pat. Once we settle the estate, I mean."

"I know. We really have grown apart, haven't we? I guess we all just got busy with our own lives and well, quite honestly, I know I didn't make much of an effort." He hung his head.

"I think we're all guilty of that," Chris admitted. "I want to enjoy being with you again even though it has been quite challenging at times."

"Truer words were never spoken," Pat said. They both forced a laugh. "Having four sisters hasn't been easy. I feel so much closer to you and Hallow than to Eve and Easter, but don't tell them I said that."

"Too much drama?"

"Yeah, among other things."

"I know. I guess I'd hoped for a little more maturity from some of us, but we're attached to our family for better or worse, I suppose," Chris replied.

"I think they're at least thinking over their squabbles," he said, coming up beside her.

She looked up at him. "Thanks." She went back to opening dresser drawers. "It's best to get this over with. I guess it's time to get rid of Mama's underwear and pajamas. She's got a lot of other stuff crammed in these drawers, too." She showed him a wad of cash.

"Goodness! I knew she always had cash on hand, but I'm surprised there's any left," Pat said. He counted the bills. "Over two hundred dollars here."

"I guess when she went to the hospital, she figured she'd come home again," Chris whispered with a sad voice.

"Yeah, Mama wouldn't have thought her life would end there," Pat agreed.

With little fanfare the three sisters entered the bedroom. "Okay! We're all ready to dive in," Eve announced. "Where do you want to start, Chris?"

Her three sisters stood side by side, smiling at her weakly.

"Let's work on going through Mama's personal stuff. Y'all can lay all her closeted clothes across the back of the couch in the den. I'm putting her drawer stuff on this bed." Chris reached into a drawer and lifted quite a few slips, turned, and put them on the bed. "You might find something in here you want although I expect these are way too big for all of us."

As Hallow and Eve looked through the pile, Pat and Easter got busy emptying the closet and the chest of drawers.

"You're right. They don't fit us, but some of them are beautiful, and the lace is gorgeous," Eve replied.

"Do you all remember when we were young and all wore slips?"

"Yes, I hated those things! Mine always hung out from under my dress," Easter said.

"And Mama or one of her friends would say, "I see your Christmas!" All the girls laughed.

"Yeah, and I hated that because I got a few extra laughs because of my name," Chris admitted.

"I think we all hated slips, but Mama made us wear them. Once I left here, though, I never wore one again unless I had on a sheer skirt."

"Well, my clothes feel so much better when they glide over a slip," Eve said. Nobody responded to that so they continued with their projects.

"Oh, look what I've found!" Hallow called out. "It's an entire box of beautiful vintage handkerchiefs." She pulled the lid off the square cardboard box to let them see the beauties. All ten of them were different patterns in pastel greens, blues, and yellows.

"Pat, can you reach that stuff on the back of that closet shelf?" Easter pointed up with her cane.

He moved over to the closet and grabbed an old suitcase. "This has to be an antique."

"Oh, I remember that old thing," Hallow called out. The dusty gray fabric suitcase had seen better days. "I doubt it would meet any of today's flight standards," she added.

"I'll take it if nobody else wants it," Eve said. They all looked at her as if she'd grown a tail. "For sentimental reasons, of course."

"Well, at least you can fill it up with things to take home and then get rid of it," Chris pointed out.

Easter suddenly grabbed Hallow's hand and studied her knuckle. "What on earth is that growth?"

"It's a *wart*, Easter," Hallow huffed. "Instead of a Prince Charming, I got peed on by a horny toad, okay?" Even though her tone was ugly, the rest of them burst into laughter.

"Oh!" Eve suddenly yelled. "I gotta pee! I'm about to wet my panties!"

More laughter ensued. It felt good to hear it throughout the house and Hallow joined in.

"Who'd want to be caught dead with that thing?" Easter called out, pointing at the luggage.

"There must be twenty pairs of shoes in here on the floor. Most of them are crushed under others," Easter said. "I know she bought lots of shoes and then got home and hated them."

"Yes, probably not many of them have been worn, but they still look beat up. She never would take anything back," Chris said, looking over the pile.

"What size are they?" They all looked at Eve.

"Size 6, I think." Hallow looked inside a pair. "Yep, 6 Medium. Anybody want them?"

They all declined.

"Pat, can you find a box to put them in? They can all go to The Salvation Army," Chris called out.

Pat soon had all the shoes bagged up and took them out to his truck. At least they were out of the way.

"I had no idea Mama had so many padded hangers. Some of them are really pretty and can be salvaged," Eve said. They turned and nodded.

"Let's go through all these pajamas and gowns and decide what to do with them," Chris advised. The four sisters gathered around the bed.

"I'm going out in the yard to see what's there. I don't want any underwear, PJs, or gowns," Pat announced.

Easter giggled. "Oh, come on, Pat. You'd be so cute in a nightgown." The door closed swiftly behind him.

"I think we can all agree to throw Mama's underwear away?"

"Yes," they said in unison.

Eve held out a large black trash bag and they stuffed it full of bras and panties.

"Some of these gowns look brand new," Hallow commented.

"I don't ever remember Mama wearing gowns. They were probably gifts she just put in the drawer." They all picked up a gown and looked it over.

"They're too big for me," Easter said.

"I like to sleep in gowns that are roomy," Hallow admitted.

"Well, take them, Hallow," Chris said.

"Wait! I might want a few, too," Eve said, studying the pile.

"They're too big for you, too, Eve. And these pajamas have seen better days. Let's just pitch them," Chris said. Eve stayed quiet and left the room while the other three crammed pajamas into a bag to go out in the trash.

Once most of the clothes were off the bed, Chris pulled some hat boxes out of a storage bench. Each hat was in its own box, tied with a ribbon. She'd leave those until later. She also placed quite a few pocketbooks on the bed, and at least thirty scarves, some in bold prints that their mother liked but she never did. She took the jewelry organizer from behind the closet door and flipped it around so they could go through it later. She could hear the others in the living room going through the other clothes, so she joined them.

"Oh my!" Hallow nearly yelled. "Why on earth did Mama keep this thing?" She held up a rose prom dress, yellowed with age. "My junior prom dress. I don't even remember my date."

"Well, Mama must have thought it was worth saving," Chris said.

"I can't for the life of me imagine why." Hallow started to toss the gown into a trash bag. "Out it goes!"

"Didn't she make it herself? You know what a fantastic seamstress she was," Chris said.

Hallow looked in the neck of the dress. "There's no tag. Maybe she *did* make it and that's why she kept it." She studied those tiny pink rosebuds made by her mother's hand. Then sadly she placed it in the yard bag.

Chris joined Eve, Easter, and Hallow, going through the pile. They stuffed many bags full of ragged, outdated, and extra-large clothes, and pitched them by the door to go into Pat's truck.

Eve went through the pockets of an unconstructed jacket and pulled out a folded paper. She opened it and started giggling and waving it.

"This coat must be ancient."

"What's *that?*"

"Just your report card from high school, Easter," Eve chortled. Easter tried to grab it but Eve was too quick for her and ran across the room, reading it aloud. "English 12 D-, Algebra F—"

"That's enough, Eve." Chris approached her sister. "Give it to Easter and let's move on."

"I never knew you made such bad grades, Easter."

"For crying out loud! I had a terrible senior year but I graduated! Don't you remember me being on medication and in traction almost the whole year?"

Eve's head dropped. "Oh, yeah. Yes, I do, Easter. I'm sorry. That was insensitive."

"Who cares about grades so long ago? Gee! You're in your sixties now so who gives a flying dip stick?" Hallow yelled at both of them. "I had some bad grades too."

Easter grabbed the report card, ripped it into tiny pieces, and threw them in the nearest trash can.

Pat came in the door and moved the trash bags outside before coming back inside. "I found an old rusty bike in the garage. The tires are rotten. Anybody want it?"

"No," the four sisters said.

"Okay, it goes in the trash too." Pat headed out to take care of it, and they could hear him talking to someone.

"Who's out there?" Hallow peeked out the window. Chris headed to the window, too, but they both scurried away as Pat stepped on the porch with the man right behind him.

"Come on in, Hal," Pat said, opening the door. "Brace yourself to meet all *four* of my sisters at once." Both men laughed.

As the man came to a stop beside Pat, his sisters lined up to greet him.

"Hal Brown, this is Eve, Hallow, Easter, and Chris."

"My pleasure, ladies," the handsome man said, nodding at each of the women. "We live on the corner and I heard y'all were back in town so my wife and I cooked up a meal for you. We know you've been busy going through things." He handed the bags to Eve and Hallow. "I hope you like spare ribs, collards, potatoes and cornbread.

And there's half a chocolate layer cake in there too."

"Wow! How nice of you," Chris called out. "It sounds divine." She walked closer while the other three took the food to the kitchen table. "So, you *are* a Brown."

"Yes, my parents lived there until their deaths and then we rented it out for years, doing a lot of repairs and updates along the way. I think I remember some of you being around before I left home."

"I'm the oldest of our bunch and I don't remember you," Chris admitted.

Charlie nodded. "That's okay. I wasn't around much. I went to a private school." He seemed embarrassed and dropped his head briefly. "Well, I hope you enjoy the food and get things done. It's never easy going through everything they accumulated. We had to do the same thing." He turned toward the door. "Nice to meet y'all … again." The sisters waved and Pat walked him out.

Bags rattled as the food came out, plates and forks appeared, and chairs were pulled back. "Let's eat! I'm starved!" Easter announced.

Eve poured them all some Pepsi and they chowed down.

They got back to the chore of going through every single item that hadn't been touched, and the afternoon flew by.

As darkness set in, Eve said, "I'm hungry again. And tired." They all looked at their watches or phones, wondering where the day had gone.

"Me too, and there's enough roast for tonight and lunch tomorrow," Chris announced.

"And there's some leftover collards and potatoes. We ate all the corn bread, though," Hallow added.

"That was mighty fine cornbread," Pat said.

Easter lowered her head to the table. "Yeah, it was." She hobbled to a chair and sat. "I'm bushed. I just can't do anything else tonight."

"I think we could all use a break," Pat added. "We've done a lot today. Let's just sit around and visit, maybe reminisce about Daddy and our childhood."

"Yeah, we can take baths and hit the sack early," Hallow said. "I'm downright lethargic."

Easter plopped into the recliner, and Eve and Hallow went to the couch. Pat started a fire to take the chill off until bedtime. Chris walked over to the big sofa and made herself a spot between her two sisters.

"We have tons to be grateful for, don't we?"

Pat sat in the glider rocker and lifted his socked feet to the matching ottoman. "My dogs are tired." They all smiled weary smiles.

"We are so blessed," Hallow said, "and sometimes I forget even though stuff happens, it's not permanent. I need to remember that."

"What's going on, Hallow?" Easter asked.

"Oh," Hallow's face flushed. "Nothing. I was just making a comment. We are blessed, aren't we?"

"Sure," Chris answered, studying her sister with skepticism. "We had two wonderful parents who stayed married to each other and we didn't have to go through all the dysfunction so many are dealing with."

"I'm happy about that," Pat chimed in. "Marriage isn't always easy, but I can't imagine children having several step-parents or live-in boyfriends. No wonder they're so confused about just about everything. I see so many sad children come to the bank with adults and they look miserable and have their faces crushed into the cell phones. Even *toddlers* have cell phones now! It's absurd!"

"Well, the parents have *their* faces in phones all the time too, and I see kids in restaurants begging for attention and not getting it. It makes me want to cry," Eve said. "I was reading the other day about how many young children now have emotional problems. It's no wonder."

"How did we get on such a sad topic?" Chris asked. They all shrugged. "Pat, did you find Daddy's fishing pole?"

"Yeah, it's not in good shape, but for sentimental reason I'd like to take it home and maybe put some oil on it and find a place to put it somewhere in the house. I was thinking about all the times he took me with him. He wanted me to learn to fish, but I preferred skipping rocks."

"You don't have an athletic bone in your body, Pat." Easter smirked at him.

"I heard that plenty when I was growing up, and you are correct." They all laughed. "I think Hallow is the only one who had any athletic ability if you call cheering a sport."

"I resemble that remark," Hallow said as they all giggled.

"Changing the subject," Eve said, "what are we doing tomorrow?"

"Well, let's go to church like we planned. Then we can finish what food is left and decide on all the small furniture like end tables, lamps, everything on the walls, the plants, and that kind of stuff. I guess it'll be time to pack it up and head to our homes," Chris offered.

"What about big items like beds, this couch, that recliner and that rocker?" Hallow pointed out.

"If we have time, we can decide on all that. We've already taken home what we post-it noted, haven't we?"

"I still have stuff here with my post-its because it was dark and nasty weather last time and my bug doesn't hold much," Easter pointed out.

"Easter, once I haul off the trash bags in my truck, I can take your things to you," Pat told her. "I'm just not sure I can get rid of them on Sunday.

I think the landfill is closed. I may have to take them to Wilmington's landfill Monday before work."

"As long as I get my choices, I don't care. Thanks, Pat."

"You betcha."

Hallow yawned and Eve followed.

"I'm going to take a shower," Eve announced, getting to her feet.

"I'm next," Easter called out.

"I'll take mine in the morning. I'm fast and won't use as much hot water as you girls."

"True enough," Chris responded. "By the way, there's so much going on in April. Can we wait until May to come back? Maybe we can get through the rest then and have warmer weather too."

"Works for me. I hope Phyllis will be coming in for a few weeks in April."

"I don't know how you do it, Pat."

"Do what, Easter?"

"Stay married but not *really* married. I mean, y'all are never together!"

Pat's face blanched. "It's complicated but we are *really* married, Easter." He stood and walked to the door, not wanting a conversation with Easter about his wife.

❀ ❀ ❀

After church the next day, they ate the roast and lemon meringue pie she'd brought.

"It's so good," Easter remarked as Eve nodded in agreement.

"I was disappointed that a visiting minister was standing in for the pastor, but glad to see some folks and sing two of Daddy's favorite hymns."

"Yeah, did you call Mrs. Hazel and request "In the Garden" and "Whispering Hope?" Chris shook her head.

"I guess it was a happy coincidence," Hallow said.

"I think it was a God thing. I *do* believe in God things," Chris told them all.

After they ate Pat said, "Since I don't plan to wear any of Mama's stuff, I'm going to round up Daddy's tools." He headed out the kitchen door and leaned back to add, "If that's okay with all of you?"

"Sure," the four sisters said in unison.

The sisters worked diligently, deciding on where articles of clothing should end up. Pat had found a huge cardboard box, and clothing now peeked over the top of it. This box was marked for "Salvation Army." Many yard trash bags bulged with items that nobody could possibly want. They had at least cleared most of their mother's personal belongings and then they spread out the pocketbooks as each picked one they wanted. Eve gathered the rest of them—most weary-looking—stating that some of her school kids could use them.

"Whoa!" Hallow called out, peering into a dark red leather pocketbook. "There's a twenty-dollar bill in here!" She waved it at them and they, too, looked through their purses in case their mother had left more bills. To their disappointment, Hallow was the only winner.

Next, they opened all the hat boxes to see what they could find. "This is like a scavenger hunt," Eve said with child-like excitement.

The six boxes contained hats their mother had designed and sewn herself, including a pink satin one that she had worn in Chris's wedding. Yellowed now, it went into the trash. Some boxes contained several small hats called pill-boxes from the days of President Kennedy's first lady, a fashion icon that all ladies in the '60s tried to emulate. None of the hats were in good shape but each sister would take a hat box home.

They completely finished with their mother's clothes and all of her accessories except her jewelry, most of it costume pieces someone had given her. The only valuable piece might be her wedding rings although the diamonds were only chips—most likely all their father could afford at the time they wed in 1941.

"She had such tiny fingers, didn't she?"

"She sure did," Hallow noticed. They all tried on the ring but it didn't fit any of them. They decided that Chris would keep it until they could all decide on what to do with it.

They loaded the items they were taking to their own homes and realized the afternoon had gone. The time had come to part again.

13: PAT

I'd found plenty of rusted tools along the garage wall and gathered them all into a canvas tarp I found at the back where Mama had potted plants after Daddy died. She had never used the tools but kept them in case someone else needed to use them for repairs around the house. With a little filing, they'd be useful again. I looked over an array of lead paint cans, most with rusty lids, and decided to go ahead and load them in my truck. They would have to be discarded at the landfill.

Once I had finished that, I went back to get Daddy's fly rod, not in great shape, but still intact. I started to put it on the truck and not say anything else about it to my sisters, but Chris had made it clear that everyone was to let the others know what they picked. I also got a six-foot metal ladder and leaned it against my truck, hoping I could take that home with me.

I went back into the house with the fly rod. Eve was the only one who had an interest in it and I asked her if she planned to fish. She said 'no' and reluctantly agreed that I could have it. I got lucky on the ladder, too, because none of my sisters had a way of taking it home. I was the only one with a truck. I was pleased with my small wins, feeling a bit silly, but having some of Daddy's things was important to me. I could remember him fishing with that rod. He was like poetry in motion. He tried to teach me the technique, but I never could get the hang of it. Just watching him catch some nice bass at the river was fun for me, and I got to take them off the hook for him.

I also remembered holding that ladder for him to climb up to trim the hedgerows with the electric clippers. Once he had climbed to the top and got the electrical cord situated, he began to cut with the powerful machine, disturbing a huge nest of hornets that came out and stung him all over the face and neck. I ran for the house, and he dropped the clippers, got down the ladder somehow and ran for the house too. I'll never forget how swollen his face was by the time he came inside. He looked like a horror movie. I know it had hurt. He said, "Son, go get my pack of cigarettes off the table." I did and watched him tear some of them open and stick the tobacco on the worst places as

Mama and I stood by in shock. It was amazing that he didn't end up in the hospital from anaphylactic shock.

14

Chris decided to make a surprise visit to Eve while she was in the Rocky Mount area on Tuesday. She rang the front bell, but Eve didn't come to the door. She walked around the side of the house, saw Eve's car and headed to the backdoor that she hadn't entered in several years. The screen door was latched, so she knocked. Then she knocked again and finally called out to her sister. While she waited, she noticed how trashy the yard was and loaded with unusual and unappealing statuary.

Eve appeared at the door, only opening it far enough to see, her eyes wide as saucers. "Wh—what are you doing here?"

"I had a DAR meeting downtown and thought I'd stop by."

"Why?"

"Do I have to have a reason? I'm your sister, for goodness sake!"

Eve twitched and danced around on her toes. "Look, the house is a mess and I'm just going out." One look at her told Chris her sister wasn't going out the way she was dressed.

"I won't stay but a minute, I promise. Open the screen door," Chris said, giving the door a snatch that brought the screen into her face. Eve backed away from the door and fled.

"I don't want you here!"

"Eve, what in the world's wrong with you?"

As Chris tried to push open the wood door, she realized that she couldn't. Her eyes moved about the small kitchen and dining room and into the den in the distance, trying to take in what she saw. With horror, she shoved on the door and made her way inside, stepping over piles of yellowed newspapers, magazines, and filth. Her mouth flew open.

"Eve? What . . . what on earth . . . Eve? You're a *hoarder?*" Chris's eyes couldn't take in the piles of mess from floor to ceiling, corner to corner. She took a step forward and nearly fell, trying to balance on top of boxes, baskets, and junk. Eve had disappeared. Chris tried to calm down, having no idea what to make of the situation or how to deal with her sister's apparent affliction. She heard Eve crying in another room and made her way slowly through the room walking on boxes and papers that barely sank and through the doorway that led into the kitchen. Eve crouched in a corner by the fridge, this room as bad or worse than the den.

"Eve, I–"

"Go away!"

"No, honey. We need to talk about this!"

"There's nothing to talk about. These are my things and I love them."

Chris worked her way around a table and chairs all piled high with stuff, knowing that this situation was serious and she had no idea what to say or do. Once she reached Eve, she simply plopped down on a foot stool and stayed quiet as her eyes wandered from the fridge to the sink filled with empty deli boxes to the stovetop not visible at all, heaped with pots and pans and things Chris could not identify. And trash. Just plain trash. Empty bags, cardboard boxes, drink cups. Newspapers, magazines. All piled high. Trash.

Rickety boxes piled all the way to the ceiling, a towering hoard just needing a tiny touch to cause an avalanche. Chris leaned back and looked toward what she remembered as the den. Dressers piled on top of dressers, paintings in frames piled up. She counted thirteen all in one heap. Immeasurable books spilled out of a bookcase on top of another bookcase. Just enough path to get through each room by stepping into heaps of no-telling-what.

She looked back across the kitchen and noticed just enough space at the microwave to open the door and pop something inside. She turned back toward the small dining table, piled precariously high with books, lamps, and all kinds of things Chris couldn't identify.

She glanced at Eve, who cowered as though she expected a scolding, shaking uncontrollably. Chris didn't have the heart to scold. Her sister looked like a small child who feared severe punishment because her secret was out. She reached over and threw her arms around her sister and they both sobbed. Once they were spent, Chris pulled Eve to her feet.

"Is the whole house like this?"

Eve put her hands over her face and stayed silent.

Chris sat down again, stunned into silence herself for a few more minutes, her mind reeling to find the right words to tell her sister.

After a few minutes she asked, "How do you bathe and find clothes?"

"I . . . I have space in the bathroom," Eve managed to say softly with a hint of a smile. "Um, I shower, use the toilet and put on makeup in there."

"What about clothes? Are they clean?"

"*Of course, they're clean!*" Eve shot out angrily.

"Okay, honey. I'm just trying to understand how you can get up, bathe, dress, go and teach every day, eat and, well, sleep."

"I have some space on the bed," Eve offered, nodding her head a little.

"How do you eat? Cook?"

"The deli is right down the street. I don't cook. And if you're wondering about the soup and bread I took to Mama's, it came from there, and it was clean!"

"Oh, I'm sure it was. I'm not questioning that." Chris fumbled attempts to help. "How long has this been going on, honey?"

Eve left out a seismic sigh and screwed up her face. "Since Matt died. I just can't get myself together. My rock is gone, you know? I totally adored him. And then Kirsten moved out and joined the Air Force."

"I know how much you loved him, honey. As much as I loved Henry." Chris stopped talking for a second, studying her sister.

"Oh, I'm sorry. I *know* you know how it feels to lose the love of your life. But you stayed so strong through it all, Chris. You seem to have a strength I just don't have."

"I'm not as strong as I appear to be, Eve."

"I started shopping, and the house filled up with stuff and Kirsten spent many nights with friends to avoid being here. I pushed her away, Chris." Eve burst into tears again.

Chris held her, not knowing how to console her. She'd always thought there was more to the

story of Kristen's sudden decision to leave. Now
she understood. Poor Kirsten lost her father and
her mother, and nobody in the family came to
her rescue. With this thought, Chris sobbed too.

"Why are you crying?"

"Because I wasn't here for you, Eve. Not
enough. I had no idea how much you needed
me. *All* of us."

"You all had your own lives. And I certainly
didn't want Mama to know. She'd have told
everybody she knows." Chris figured Eve was
right about that. Their mother couldn't keep a
secret to save her life.

"And not only that, she would have thrown it
in my face every chance she got."

"Maybe not, Eve. Cut her a little slack. After
all, she lost her spouse too."

"Well, you know how she is . . . was," Eve
whispered.

"So, has collecting stuff helped?"

"Well, not exactly." She flung away from me.
"I knew you wouldn't understand. I don't want
you here, Chris." She put both hands on her hips
in defiance.

"You know this isn't healthy, right?"

Eve's face turned red and she roared toward
the den, knocking some piles over into the small
path behind her. "I want you to go! And don't tell
anybody about this. It's nobody's business but
mine!"

"I'll go," Chris said. "But Eve, Matt wouldn't want you to live like this. I'm sure of it. He loved you enough to want you to find happiness again."

Eve's anger turned to trembling sobs. "P…please leave," she eked out.

Chris climbed over the piles and followed the tiny path to the backdoor. Before she walked out, she turned back toward Eve. "I want you to know I love you, sis," she called out and closed the door behind her, knowing this was all she would think about on her long drive back to Morehead City.

15: CHRIS

Stunned by what I'd witnessed, I turned into my driveway at home, not knowing how I'd driven all the way from Rocky Mount in a daze. That in itself was scary. I'd been on auto-pilot since I left Eve's house. I felt numb, my head in a fog, it spun through the piles of junk and filth that engulfed her house. I knew I'd handled Eve all wrong. I'd never been around a hoarder. I realized that my fingers throbbed from the long drive in cold weather. And once again, I had forgotten to put on my copper gloves.

Inside the house, I rubbed my hands together, locked up, threw my purse on the counter, and slunk off to run a tub of fragrant bath water in hopes of ending the funk that had attached itself to me. Once in the tub, I soaked away not only oily skin but also some of the day's stress—some, not all. Once I felt squeaky clean, I rose and stepped out, wrapping myself in a warm fluffy towel even though my thoughts were far from squeaky clean.

Eve. Poor sweet Eve. What had happened to my sister? Had grief taken her over the edge? She'd said little except to tell me to get out and keep my mouth shut. But she needed help. I pulled on a robe and slid my feet into slippers before padding into the kitchen to make a BLT and a strong cup of decaf.

I surfed through TV channels until I stopped at a show about hoarding. If I could stand to watch it, maybe I'd find clues and a way to help my sister. As I watched family and professionals intervene with two different hoarders, tears rained down my face hard enough that I couldn't keep them wiped away. Both hoarders had experienced traumatic events. One was a lady whose son had committed suicide. The other had experienced a divorce after her husband cheated on her with her best friend. I realized that I was holding my breath and exhaled strong enough to send a ripple across my coffee, now cold. I turned off the TV and lamps and headed for bed, hoping that I could sleep without nightmares.

❀ ❀ ❀

I greeted the day with a headache of seismic magnitude, the pain sensation akin to an earthquake—a migraine! I lifted my head up and over the bed far enough to spew the tsunami of vomit into a nearby wastebasket. No doubt my day would be spent in bed. I gently rolled over and tried to sleep the pain away.

16: EVE

I had fallen hard and fast in love with Matthew Rockford and devoted myself to him. He and our daughter, Kirsten, were my top priorities. They were my everything. My life. And then suddenly Matt was gone and Kirsten was grown and out of the house. And I had at least partially folded in on myself, only awakening when I was in the classroom with my labs and test tubes, guiding students through experiments with as much enthusiasm as I could muster. During school hours I had a respite. But each day when I got home, my world would turn dark and bleak as soon as I opened the door. I realized after several months of being numb that I had accumulated *things*. Nothing special at all. Nothing I needed. Just *things* I had gone out and bought to fill the hours until bed time as if they would make me feel again.

Feel something. *Anything*! Kirsten had stopped hanging around the house after school because she couldn't stand the way I'd let the house go. She was embarrassed to bring friends over. And who could blame her?

And at what point had I become such a slob? Why hadn't I thrown out the trash? The empty pizza boxes and drink cups? I'd sunk to a level I couldn't even imagine.

Lost. That's what I was. Just miserably lost. Over time most people seemed to put the grief farther and farther back in their emotions. I never could. I just never could.

And now Chris had shown up and discovered my secret. Even though I'd told her to get out and stay quiet about what she'd seen, I knew I couldn't count on her to do that. She'd want to interfere, to intervene, and I just wasn't ready for any of that. I knocked books off my bed and crawled in, not wanting to endure any more of this day. I felt like a busted can of biscuits. Glad tomorrow was Sunday, I could once again pull myself back together before Monday.

17

The following weekend, the five once again walked through the old house, deciding how to rid it of the furniture and other smaller items. Chris looked over at Eve but had no intention of spilling her secret, at least not yet. She hoped Eve would do that herself when she was ready. She had noticed, though, that Hallow just wasn't herself. Always the optimist and a flirt, the sparkle seemed gone. Deepening lines on her face held worry. She had become so distant and she wore sadness like a wool blanket. Chris had always been closer to this sister since they were two years apart and the oldest of the children. Now Hallow avoided looking Chris in the eye whenever possible, a good indicator something crucial was amiss. When they were alone, out of earshot from the rest of the world, Chris broached the subject.

"What's going on with you, Hallow?" Her sister shrugged. "Well, I know something's going on because you don't usually avoid me. You seem so sad. Please let me help you."

Hallow's eyes filled with tears. "There's nothing you can do, sis."

"Surely, that's not true."

Hallow looked away as if she wanted to fall through the floor and not have this conversation. Chris remained silent until Hallow sighed deeply, looked around to see where the others were and looked her in the eye.

"I've lost everything, Chris."

"What do you mean?"

"*Everything.* You know I've never been lucky in love." She let out a mock laugh. "This last romance cost me my life savings, all the money in my checking account, most of the furniture in the house. All I have left is the house itself, and it's practically empty. I'm living on social security and a wedding once in a while."

Chris couldn't find words as she sat in shock and looked at Hallow, who had placed her head in both hands in misery.

"How did he manage to do all that?"

"I had a wedding in Asheville, and he didn't want to go with me, so I left him at the house. How did I know he'd planned all that? I had no inkling, Chris. Richard had stayed over lots of nights, and I guess his whole purpose had been to rip me off when an opportunity arose. He got my checking and savings account numbers and cleaned me out. He loaded a moving van with my most expensive furniture. By the time I drove from Asheville to Raleigh, he'd left with all of it. When I got home and opened the door, I just couldn't believe my eyes. I ran to my closest neighbor's house. She said she saw a big truck over there, but just figured I was moving. It's not like any of my neighbors are close friends, so she had no idea."

"How long ago was this, Hallow?"

"Right after Mama died and before we met at the old place for the first time."

"And you've carried this burden alone all this time? I'm speechless. I'm so sorry, Hallow. Why didn't you call one of us? Why didn't you say something when we were together?"

"What was there to say? What were you going to do, Chris? He's long gone."

"Call the police? Find a trail or something."

"I did call the police. We found out his real name wasn't even Richard Davenport. He told me he'd recently returned from active duty, and I bought it all. There's no trail to follow. The police said he'd used an alias."

"How could he just walk in and take it all? Aren't there some safeguards against that?" Hallow shrugged. "Well, I'm going to ask Pat if there's any way to trace this."

"No! I don't want anyone to know how stupid I've been."

"Not even Pat?"

"Not even Pat. Don't say a word."

"I think you're making a mistake there, Hallow."

"What's another mistake at this point? I'm ruined, Chris. My whole wedding business is ruined."

"Why?" Chris took her sister's hands. "Listen to me, Hallow. Your career is not over. You've always been determined and smart and talented. You have so much experience, and you have a pile of clients that can refer you to other brides. Don't let that slime ball ruin your life and take your joy."

Hallow dissolved into tears. Chris threw her arms around her, realizing that she had two sisters—maybe three—who seemed emotionally fragile. And more to the point, perhaps all five of them were on shaky ground.

18: CHRIS

Most of the past three nights I'd stayed awake worrying about two of my sisters. Now I slapped at the alarm clock and missed just enough to off-balance it so it fell onto the floor. Still the annoying buzzer continued to pierce my delicate ears as I dropped from the bed to pick it up.

Both Hallow and Eve sought happiness in the wrong ways. Eve in things and Hallow in bad relationships. Both of them needed strong support from the family. I pondered the best way to handle each situation. Like I was a shrink or something. Pat was almost always oblivious—or was it indifferent—to what was going on around him. Easter, until recently, had spent most of her time and energy poking at our emotional sores just to watch them fester. Maybe I was being unfair to them, but here I was, stuck in the middle again, and I wasn't singing the song. I made my decision, although I knew it wouldn't be popular. The phone rang five times before I heard my brother's voice.

"Pat, this is Chris."

"Hey, sis. I'm right in the middle of a big loan. Can I call you back?"

"We need to talk. Can I meet you somewhere after work?"

"Um, sure. Where are you?"

"I'm at home right now but I'm heading your way if you have time."

"Sure. How about I order some pizza and you come to the house about six?"

"Sounds great."

Even though Pat lived in Wilmington where he worked, and Chris lived in Morehead City, she arrived at his house before he did, so she sat in her SUV with the heated seat on until he drove past her into his garage. Chris studied her brother as he exited with a huge pizza box and walked toward her, loosening his tie. Her brother was one fine-looking man—a good man, as far as she knew—spotless reputation, adored no doubt by women everywhere and envied by men. She hopped out and followed him into the house, clicking her key fob to lock her Toyota. They hugged and shrugged out of their coats.

"Let me hang these up and we'll eat while it's hot."

"I'll fix us something to drink," Chris said on the way to the fridge.

"I made some green tea last night," he called back from the hallway.

Chris got glasses, added ice, and poured them both sweet green tea. She looked around the beautiful downstairs, admiring the high-end furnishings, paintings, and how neat and clean Pat kept the place for a man living alone. Although, she had to admit that Pat had always been neat, far neater than she and her sisters had ever been. She wondered how he remained faithful to a wife who was gone ninety percent of their marriage. Yet she felt certain he had never wandered. They ate and caught up on their lives, Chris wanting to wait until later to discuss her reason for coming.

"Well," Pat said, finishing off the last of the pizza, "I assume this is important since you drove this far."

Chris nodded. "Yeah, it is. By the way, that was delicious. Thanks for picking it up."

"No problem. I was planning to get myself one anyway. Even though I know how to cook some things, it's no fun when I'm alone most of the time." His head drooped.

Chris shifted and looked Pat in the eye. "Since you brought it up, can I ask you a personal question?"

"Sure, I guess."

"Don't you get hit on, you know, by beautiful women?"

He blushed. "Sometimes, yeah." He backed his chair from the table and stood.

"With Phyllis gone so much, how do you stay faithful?"

"Of all my sisters, you're the one I'd least expected to ask that question. This conversation calls for coffee. Want some?" Chris nodded. He headed to the counter and put a pod in the Keurig before turning back to her. "I always thought I'd end up a bank president, you know? But at this point I guess J.D. Withers will stay until they take him out on a gurney." He let out a heavy sigh.

"There are other banks. Have you ever considered transferring to another one? I mean, there's one on nearly every corner in this town."

"Yeah, but I'm a creature of habit, kind of set in my ways now and not sure I'd want to change at this point. Should have done it years ago," Pat admitted. "I guess I got lazy. Phyllis has always made more money, and that rubs me the wrong way, but I haven't made a move to change things." He sipped and looked up at Chris. "What's with all the questions, sis?"

"I'm just concerned that you're alone so much."

"Well, you're alone too, Chris."

"Yeah, but Henry died. Phyllis is still living. You still love her, right?"

"Yeah, I guess."

"You *guess*? Pat, you'd better know for sure," Chris said, patting his arm.

"This conversation is making me uncomfortable. You drove all this way to drill me about my marriage?"

"No—"

"I know our relationship seems strange to the rest of you, but it's always worked." He dropped his head. "I can't tell you I'm happy with this arrangement, but I knew Phyllis was career-minded before I married her years ago. I guess I thought she'd get tired of traveling and stay put. Didn't happen." He drained his coffee cup. "That's why I need to focus on her while she's home or I'm not sure we can last much longer."

"I didn't come here to pry, Pat. I was trying to make polite conversation. I apologize if I got all up in your personal life." Chris reached for his hand. "But look, you've got your years in. Why don't you retire and travel with her? See the world?" She hoped her voice carried a lighter tone.

"I've considered that, but Phyllis and I are like strangers now. It's a strained relationship at best. I'm not sure she'd want me around. I *do* know that I've got to spend time with her. We need to have a serious discussion about our marriage and go from there."

"Huh," was Chris's only comment. She stood and took her cup to the kitchen counter. He followed. "I wish you the best with that, Pat." He nodded.

"I'm doing all I know to do on this end. I go to church every Sunday unless I'm out of town or under the weather. I usually go on Wednesday nights too to support Wayne, our pastor. He's my best friend, and I've talked to him about all this. It keeps my mind from wandering off down the wrong paths."

"I didn't know that. How wonderful to have a friend in the ministry."

"Yeah, he's been through so much in his life and he's taught me how to study—not just read— the Bible. And pray. I thought I knew how to pray but I think my prayers are so much more meaningful now. And that brings with it lots of peace of mind." He shook his head slowly and smiled. "I have a greater inner peace now. So, whatever happens, I'm going to be fine, I think."

"Wow! I'm so proud of you. Mama and Daddy would be proud too," Chris said, throwing her arms around him.

"When I married, I took my vows seriously, Chris. I hope she did too." He looked away.

"Do you have doubts?"

"No, not really, but I know she works with lots of men in her line of work. I think I know where her heart is, though. And we talk at night, so I think I'd detect a problem if it were there."

"Well, both of you are wonderful people and I hope it all works out well."

"Is that seriously why you drove all this way? Do *you* have doubts? Have you heard anything I need to know?"

"No, not at all! Rest your mind on that issue. I just think you're such a fine man. That's all. Even if you are my brother." They both laughed, and Chris shifted her weight. "I didn't mean for the conversation to get so personal and off track. I'm actually here about Hallow."

"Then let's sit in the den where it's more comfortable." She followed him and plopped on the champagne-colored sofa while he turned on the gas logs. "It should warm up fast." He took a seat in a leather navy recliner and put his hands on his knees. "So, what's up?"

"First of all, Pat, she's going to be upset that I'm telling you this."

"Telling me what?" His eyes bored into hers.

Chris sat up straight and folded her hands in her lap. "Hallow is in a real mess, Pat. You know what a romantic soul she is?" He nodded. "Well, she picked the wrong one this time. He cleaned her out."

"Cleaned her out?"

"Yeah, all the furniture not nailed down, and you know she had some gorgeous pieces."

He nodded his head again.

"This man—he went by the name Richard— swept her off her feet. She let him sleep over countless times, and then she left to do a wedding on the other side of the state. By the time she got home from Asheville, he'd left for parts unknown with all of it. She opened the door to nothing but some of her clothes and a toothbrush. When she questioned a neighbor, she said he backed a van up and loaded it. The neighbor figured she was moving and never questioned it.

"Please tell me he didn't get her money."

"Every penny she'd saved all her life, Pat."

He jumped from his chair and banged the recliner arm. "For heaven's sake! I've tried to tell her not to be so trusting!"

"I know; we all have. This guy really did a number on her. Somehow, he got all of it. How could that happen, Pat?"

"Unless she was foolish enough to make him an authorized signee on her account, he took it illegally. He probably had access to her checkbook, social security card, credit cards and PINs. He could easily go through her purse and get that."

"I don't think she would make him a signee, but he could have been in her purse while she was out or sleeping."

"Probably."

"But wouldn't somebody at the bank become suspicious of such a large amount? I think it was thousands, maybe as much as eighty thousand dollars."

"I'd be willing to bet he took her whole checkbook or maybe an extra book in her desk and then went to quite a few banks to cash them, just under an amount that would seem suspicious, committing check fraud, and forging her signature. He could get quite a lot using ATMs too."

"I just can't believe she's lost it all."

"I'll try to talk to Hallow and get more details. Maybe he mentioned other names or where he's from or something to track him with. Did she go to the police?"

"Yes, but they haven't found out a darn thing to help her."

Pat exhaled heavily, shaking his head.

"She's going to be upset with me," Chris said, "but I'm hoping you can help."

"She'll get over being upset, Chris. You did the right thing. I have a friend who investigates insurance fraud. I'll call him and see if he has any ideas on how to proceed."

"Okay."

"This guy's more than likely basking in the sun on a remote island in the Caribbean somewhere enjoying the money Hallow saved all her adult life.

A total piece of garbage! And I'd be willing to bet Hallow wasn't his first victim."

"And probably not his last one." Chris stood and hugged her brother. "I've got to get home, but thanks for the pizza. I'll call Hallow and confess to telling you. That way she can chew me out and be ready for your call."

Pat nodded and walked me to the SUV. "I'll wait a day or two or maybe drive up there this weekend."

"No, we're supposed to meet at the old home place Saturday morning. Remember? I think I'll go Friday night," Chris added as she opened her door, got in, and buckled up.

"I'm glad you reminded me. I guess I can talk to her then."

Chris drove home, relieved that she wasn't the only one who knew Hallow's situation. However, she still harbored Eve's hoarding secret, not yet sure what to do about it.

19: PAT

After Chris left, conversations lingered in my mind. The one about Hallow being ripped off, and also the one about my poor excuse for a married life. I had to admit I was lonely. Yes, that's what I was. Lonely. Sick and tired of being alone every night when I got home, spending weekends alone unless I went out to dinner or a movie with a friend. Being invited over to neighbors' cookouts always left me the odd man out and isolated, even though I did appreciate the occasional invitation.

And it wasn't about having a sexual partner at my age either. It was about having another person in the house. Someone to come home to. Another person I *loved*. While Phyllis circumnavigated the planet, I stayed put in Wilmington. In the same bank where I started forty years ago. I loved the beaches when we were younger. Now I rarely even rode down to Carolina Beach or Wrightsville to look at the ocean. I should probably grab a sandwich some days after work and just go down and walk on the pier and let the briny breeze rustle my hair. Get some sun and fresh air. But I'd felt even lonelier when I did that months ago.

Monotony had taken over my life, I now realized. I sighed with dejection. So maybe trying to help Hallow would keep my mind off Phyllis on the other side of the world and keep my rotten attitude from ruining my life, such as it was. At least for a few hours. I shucked off my dress shirt and headed for the shower, hoping it would put me in a better frame of mind before we reconvened at the old house.

20

Conflict started as soon as all five of them arrived.

"Why are *you* always in charge, Chris?"

"Because I'm the oldest. First born. Back in the day I could have kept it all for myself."

Pat stood. "And even further back than that, the only male got it all. Quit squabbling like a child." This time he glanced around at all of them and let his eyes fall on Easter.

Chris stomped across the room to her youngest sister, her face red with fury. "Just because you're a miserable person doesn't mean you have the right to make all the rest of us miserable. But you *do*," Chris erupted with a nasty tone. "I'm miserable. Hallow's miserable. Eve's miserable, and if Pat stayed around you long enough, he'd be miserable too." She got in Easter's face. "You are this family's fang, Easter."

"What do you mean by that?"

"You take every gesture, every word, every deed, and try to poison it. Yes, you *do*! You attack at every turn. I'm sick of it and sick of you!" The two sisters stared at each other in a fury.

"Are you happy now? *No?* Well, who cares, Easter? We have tried all our adult lives to do what you wanted, to be 'friends' with you because you didn't have anybody else, to be miserable company for *you*. I dread every single time I have to be around you. Do you *hear* me?"

"That's enough, Chris," Pat said, pulling her away from their whimpering youngest sister.

"Quit sniping at each other!" He glared at both of them.

"That...that's the meanest, vilest thing anybody's ever said to me, Chris. And *you?* Of all people?" Easter seemed to fold in on herself and dropped down on the ottoman as Eve ran to her. Stunned into silence, they watched Chris head for the door and slam it hard behind her, having never seen their oldest sister in a rage.

Pat hovered over them, his dark brows furrowed. "Does every word from your mouth have to be negative, Easter? Do y'all have any idea how lucky the five of us are? *Do* you? We're so fortunate to have all had the same two parents that stayed together and loved each other all their

lives. How many of our friends can say the same?"
Easter grappled with the chair's arm and her cane
and stood uncomfortable in her own skin. Hallow,
Eve and Easter stared at him for a second and
shifted their eyes down and away from his. "Give
them and this process the respect it deserves."
With that, Pat walked outside to find Chris on a
garden bench, sobbing with her head in her hands.
She didn't look up as he approached and cleared
his throat.

He stood behind her. "Rather harsh, don't you
think?"

She cupped her fingers over her forehead. "I
sh-sh-ouldn't have done that. But I'm just so sick
and tired of all the digs and complaints, Pat. Easter
brings my anger to the surface, and I've been
pretty good at suppressing it, but I just blew a
gasket this time."

"You're her favorite target, Chris. I suppose
she thinks of you as the boss of us."

Pat came around and sat down beside her.
"You're the solidifying force in our family. The
strong leader we need. But you and Easter just
rub each other the wrong way."

"Yeah, enough to start a fire." She sighed. "I
don't feel strong. I'm tired, Pat. So tired. And on
top of that, I now feel wretched for blowing up
at her."

"Well, don't. You pretty much said what we've
all felt for years. I guess it had to come out sooner

or later. And I also realize I don't get nearly as much flak from her as the rest of you. *You* especially. I'll try to do a better job of defending you." He put his arm around her and pulled her closer. "I guess you've got some of Mama in you after all."

Chris pulled away from him. "Well, that helps a lot. My goodness! I don't want to be like Mama."

"I didn't mean that you're *like* her. Mama could sometimes have a polarizing personality. She manipulated us, especially you, Chris. And she pitted us against each other. I'm old enough to remember the verbal abuse she saved for an audience."

"Oh, Pat, she could be pleasant for hours and as soon as someone else came in, she'd turn mean and insult me in one way or another. Sometimes my hair, sometimes my makeup, sometimes my weight. It's all etched in my memory with deep grooves." Tears stung her face.

"I know." Pat sighed. "I think Easter must have gotten some of Mama's disposition, and her accident made it worse. She's so full of bitterness. I guess we need to finish up here, wish each other well, and get back to our own lives. It's always you who takes charge and feels responsible, Chris. If you'd give me a chance…and Hallow…we could be helpful."

Chris wiped her face and turned to him. "I know. I'm bad for taking charge, but as the oldest and the Executor of the Estate, I feel in this case

I have to." She shuffled up and hugged her brother again. "I guess I'd better go make things right with Easter." He nodded and walked with her back inside.

"Where's Easter? I need to apologize," Chris said.

"Not today, Chris," Eve said. "She left."

"What? In this weather?"

"I'm afraid so," Hallow added.

"Oh, no. If anything happens to her, it's my fault! I need to call her."

Pat took his sister's hand. "Let me call her later, after she's home. She won't answer for you anyway. Maybe not for me, either."

"Right," said Chris in a whisper, shaking her head. "Right."

He turned to his three sisters. "Look, I'm worn out and stressed out. I'm heading home. There's nothing here I want this bad." With that, he walked out.

21: CHRIS

I couldn't stop thinking about Easter. My mind traveled back to what I'd said. I cringed. My heart slid into the pit of my stomach, causing an uncomfortable heaviness that lingered well into the night. I was supposed to be the level-headed sister, the one respected by all my siblings. Losing control in front of all of them was bad enough, but what on earth had I done to Easter? Had I permanently ruined our relationship? Had I broken her spirit? Could she ever forgive me?

Earlier in the day I had called Pat to see if he'd talked with her. All five calls had gone straight to voicemail. I texted him, and he didn't respond. Perhaps he was tied up with bank issues, but I needed some relief, knowing that I had to talk to Easter and the rest of them and apologize.

After dark I decided to call Easter and got her voicemail too.

I'm so sorry,
I finally texted.
Please find it in your
heart to forgive me.

I didn't get a response. Later I swigged a glass of wine but it didn't help. I knew I'd toss and turn all the miserable night.

Sometime during the night my cell phone buzzed. I reached over to see who'd sent a text at this hour.

Where's God's peace now?

Easter's text struck a nerve. She might as well have slapped me hard with the palm of her hand. But she was right.

God is disappointed in me,
I texted back,
and I am very disappointed in myself.

I stared at the phone for several minutes until I realized she wasn't going to respond to my admission. I threw off the covers and got up, padding to the kitchen to pop a pod in the Keurig.

In some ways I felt sorry for Easter. Well, actually, in *many* ways. Even though she had made poor choices in high school, she'd paid for them many times over the years with pain. Not just physical pain, but also emotional distress. She seemed to have a hatred for everything and took it out on those closest to her. Her family. I'd never heard her mention having social friends and never heard of her dating anyone. She had to be miserable. I guess what got me and probably everyone else, is that she took swings at us like we caused the problem. If you do that to people long enough, they'll avoid you if there's any way possible.

I snugged my knees into a pillow and prayed that Easter would somehow resolve how she dealt with her issues. I had to pray that I would also be a kinder, more considerate older sister.

22: EASTER

My efforts to act better always seemed to betray me. I still lashed out harshly to my family. Some of the conflicts across my life I knew had left deep scars. Emotional scars. It's like I'd been taken over by the devil himself and I couldn't do anything about it. I didn't want to be mean, but I think people *think* I'm mean. I hate myself! So, there it was: a full admission of the root of the matter. And I could continue to wallow in self-hatred and pity or do something about it. I just didn't feel like I could tackle it alone. And I *was* alone. *Always*. Alone. But I'd been alone most of my adult life. No dating. No relationships with the opposite sex. No sex. Nothing new there. I guess at least I hadn't loved and then buried a husband like Chris and Eve had. Maybe then being alone was a blessing?

My mind went to Chris. She had really shocked me with her words and in front of the rest of them! I was infuriated and stormed out and drove home, mad at all of them because none of them came to my defense. Pat had even torn into me and then went outside to comfort Chris! Maybe I deserved what I got. Okay, yes, I *did* deserve it. I'd just never known Chris to attack like that. Apparently, my siblings agreed with her. I just needed to be alone and pity my poor excuse of a life.

Feeling guilty, my mind went from Chris to Eve. They had both lost husbands who adored them, and even though they died, at least my sisters had been someone else's reason for living. I've never had that. Not even close! It wasn't that I resented either of them. My goodness. I loved my sisters. I wasn't sure how to define the feelings I had. 'Better to have loved and lost than never to have loved at all'—, but was that really true? Eve couldn't seem to move on, but Chris seemed to be fine, or she was better at keeping her feelings intact than I was. Hallow, on the other hand, wanted so much to find someone, but it never lasted. That had to be tough to deal with too. She was the gorgeous sister and had always exuded confidence, but I could tell that had waned a bit. I knew I behaved badly, but it's so ingrained in me now that I can't seem to find my way out of the bitterness. I slumped into a chair, exhausted from self-analysis and sighed deeply. Soon enough we would be thrown together again and have to resolve our situation.

23

May

"I want us all to go to Mama and Daddy's church together again before we close up the house," Chris announced. "Mama's birthday is on Mother's Day this year. Do you think you can make it?"

"Really? May 11th?" had been the response from all of them as they all agreed.

"So, let's do it then and try to finish up so we don't have to keep going there," Easter added as if she had something else to do. "The longer we drag it out, the more depressing it is with every trip." She and Chris hadn't spoken since the last time they were at the old house.

Chris was starting to feel the same way, more depressed with every attempt to finish this horrendous chore. Guilt niggled at her every day

since she unloaded on Easter, but distance had
probably been for the best. Maybe they could at
least be civil this time.

Chris talked Eve into going to Atkinson after
school on Friday before the others arrived on
Saturday. Once they settled in with their bags and
some ready-made food, they took a walk around
the property to see just what all had to be sold or
sorted out that none of them could use. The
grapevines would remain for anyone to pick even
if the house didn't sell. Chris wondered if it was
even fit to put on the market. None of them
wanted to spend money on fixing it up.

As they circled back toward the house, the sky
blushed right above the trees and Chris decided it
was time to tell Eve, who had become distant,
about her idea. "Eve, we need to talk."

"If it's about my collections, I don't think so,"
Eve said, looking where she stepped.

Chris tried not to grimace at Eve for using
"collections" to describe her hoarding. "I need to
share something with you . . . about Hallow."

Eve threw her head up. "Have you blabbed to
her about my messy house?"

Chris shook her head, knowing the house was far more than "messy" could ever cover. "No, I haven't blabbed, as you call it. But Eve, she's in a real mess. Before we all talk in a group, I thought you needed to know how needy she is."

"*Needy?* She certainly isn't needy in any way."

"Yeah, I'm afraid she is." Chris stepped onto the front porch and sat down on the swing after checking to make sure it could hold her weight. Eve perched on the porch's rail.

"So, what's up with Hallow?"

Chris kicked off for a gentle swing. "Well, you know she's had a number of men in her life."

"Far more than the rest of us put together, I'm sure."

"This last one cleaned her out while she was in Asheville. I mean everything but her clothes and makeup." Chris let the swing stop and made eye contact with her sister.

"Everything she owned? Even those gorgeous pieces of furniture and linens and textiles I'd kill for?"

"All gone. He cleaned out her bank accounts too, all of her life's savings. She's devastated."

"Her money too?"

"Every dime," Chris emphasized.

Eve shrunk down onto the swing beside Chris. "That's awful."

They sat there in silence for a few minutes, lost in their thoughts.

"She's living in a shell of a house with no furniture and not much money to buy anything with. Fortunately, he didn't vandalize the house before he left. She has her social security, but that's it. With her wedding planner business, she basically has no retirement to lean on. She'll probably have no choice but to sell that gorgeous house. I just thought you should know."

Eve stayed quiet and Chris eventually toddled inside to shower.

The next morning Chris and Eve ate bagels and cream cheese with coffee after they'd dressed and were on the porch when Pat and Easter pulled up in the yard, followed by Hallow, who wedged her Acadia between his truck and the VW.

"Say nothing," Chris warned Eve, who followed behind her to greet them all.

Easter hobbled toward the house in the loudest jeans Chris had ever seen.

"Please tell me you brought some more clothes for church."

"Don't you like these jeans?" Easter smirked at Chris.

"Not really. They belong on a teenager, not a sixty-something," Chris said putting her hands on her hips. Easter always knew how to push her buttons.

Easter laughed. "You're so old-fashioned, Chris. This is the style now. And most of these bright patterns are tights which I *don't* wear. I don't see anything wrong with these."

The jeans were hot pink background with yellow and purple flowers all over. *Big* flowers. Chris shook her head, deciding not to say anymore. She looked down at her own drab jeans and green shirt, sighed and walked toward Eve, noticing how tiny she looked in the black jeans she wore. Hallow's jeans were somewhere between denim blue and turquoise, but she donned an orange sweater that made a bold look, typical of Hallow. Pat wore dark trousers, a checked shirt, and a sweater, all prepped out as usual. He ran with the preppies in high school and still dressed that way, but who could complain?

"Wow! I'm so glad it's warmer and sunnier this time," Hallow said, hugging her sisters before heading to Pat and Easter to do the same as if nothing could dampen her spirit.

"Did you bring church clothes?"

"Yes, didn't we all?"

"I think so," Chris said, "although Easter swears she'll wear pants."

"That's okay," Hallow said, "even the Southern Baptists have softened their dress code."

"I don't blame her either with all those scars," Eve added. The others nodded and they all went inside.

The five pulled and piled items until they were tired and had cleared the table and its chairs enough to rest and eat lunch.

"I made lasagna soup in my crockpot at home and brought it and plugged it in. It should be nice and hot," Chris said.

"So that's what smells divine," Hallow said, taking in a deep sniff.

"I passed a bakery on the way and got four loaves of bread," Pat said. "What we don't eat today we can toast in the morning."

"Yummy! Where are the bowls and spoons?" Eve headed to the cabinets and brought back five mix-matched bowls and spoons.

"Do we have butter? I want some on my bread," Easter called out. Chris nodded.

"I guess we need to make eating stuff the last things to divide up and take out," Eve said.

"You're right," Chris said, studying what remained in the cabinets.

"I'm digging in," Pat announced. "I had a green smoothie for breakfast and it's gone."

"A smoothie? You don't need to lose weight, Pat," Hallow said, giving him a quick body scan.

"I drink them for all the nutrition, and I usually eat the other two meals. It works well with the wife gone *ninety-nine* percent of the time." The four sisters noticed a sour tone in his voice.

"Good news! This time we have hot water and so we'll leave the towels and washcloths until tomorrow afternoon and then whoever takes them can wash them." Chris hoped her comment focused them on their bowls of soup.

"Some of them feel like they'll exfoliate all the skin off my body," Easter commented. They all laughed because their mother seldom used the clothes dryer or fabric softener, preferring to hang them on the clothesline outside, and indeed, they were rough on the skin.

"Chris," Eve said, patting her hand, "this might be the best soup I've ever tasted. I want the recipe."

"Me too," the others chimed in.

"I'll send it to you," Chris told them. "I basically throw things in a big pot."

"Oh, by the way," Pat said after finishing off his soup, "since I'm the only one with a truck, I'll take all the big stuff and deliver it to whoever gets it. If we can decide some of that this weekend—like bookcases, tables, chairs, and such—I can take some on out of here when I leave tomorrow."

"That's a great idea, Pat. That way none of us will have to get someone with a truck to come and get them." Chris said.

"Yeah, but we live so far apart, that's a lot on you, Pat."

"I don't mind a bit, Hallow. I'll just work out a time to take stuff to each of you." He winked and stood to get another piece of bread and another ladle of soup.

They decided who would get large outdoor items like the deck furniture, the front porch swing, and cushions, the rolling storage bin, the bird feeder, and the bird bath and stand. There were just enough birdhouses around the yard for each of them to have one. Chris got the red ladybug, Easter got the pastel one that looked like the season for which she was named, Eve got the green tower, Hallow the copper-topped octagon and Pat a bluebird house.

"What about the wind chimes? I love the deep sound of them," Hallow said.

"I don't want them," Pat and Chris said in unison. They looked over at Eve, who hesitated and then at Easter, who came and looked them over.

"Nah, you take them, Hallow," the youngest sister said with a smile. "How about all the garden flags? Most of them look worn out and faded."

"I don't want any of those either," Pat responded.

"Me either. You girls get what you want and we'll discard the rest of them," Chris said.

Exhausted, they all bedded down not long after dark and slept well. When Chris's eyes popped open and she realized the sun had risen, she eased out of bed to attend to her bladder. Once done, she checked her watch and headed to the kitchen in her pajamas to put on some coffee. If they were going to be on time for church, they needed to eat, bathe, dress and get there no later than a quarter of eleven o'clock or they'd be ushered to the front pew.

"Good morning," Pat said, letting out a big yawn. "Did you sleep well?"

"I did. I didn't move once my head hit the pillow. I hope I didn't snore and keep Hallow awake."

They turned when they heard slippers padding across the floor. "No, if you snored, I didn't hear you. Who knew going through all the possessions in this house would be so tiring?" Hallow flipped her long hair to loosen tangles.

"I think part of it is emotionally draining, knowing this is the end of an important time in our lives." Pat sounded like a philosopher.

"Coffee's ready," Chris announced. "I'll see if the other girls are awake."

"We're coming," they said in unison. "The smell of coffee woke us."

"Good, because we have to take turns in the bathroom and get ready for church. You know where we'll have to sit if we're late."

"I am not sitting on the front row," Easter said.

"Do you think the church still has that many people?" Eve asked.

"Well, we don't know," Chris responded.

"I did a wedding there last year, and the place filled up," Hallow chimed in. "But, of course, this is Mother's Day, so I don't know."

"It filled up for Mama's funeral too," Easter added.

"Hey, I took a shower last night, and I only have to shave and I'm done in there. Can I go first?"

"I like that little silver shadow you've got, Pat. Don't shave," Easter said.

"Nah, I can't go to church looking like a slob."

"When have you ever looked like a slob?" Chris put her hands on her hips.

"Yeah!" Pat's other sisters chimed in. He blushed, shrugged, and took his coffee with him.

The sisters managed to get ready, do makeup and hair and line up on the porch. "I wish we had somebody to take our picture. All of us together for the last time on this porch," Eve said. They all nodded sadly.

"I doubt we get it all done this weekend. We'll be back."

"Yeah, but probably not dressed up like we are now," Chris said.

"Let's grab our phones and take a few pictures at least," Hallow insisted. They all agreed and posed.

The five of them gathered in front of the steep cement steps of the Atkinson Baptist Church. Chris wore a solid turquoise dress with three-quarter-length sleeves that slipped over her lithe body smoothly. She had earrings but no necklace with her black shoes. Eve wore a pink mid-calf dress and brown shoes with understated earrings and necklace. Easter had on black slacks and a white print peasant blouse with her black shoes. Hallow's long red hair flowed over a black knit jersey dress, and she had added pearl earrings and necklace Her shoes were a reddish tint. Pat donned a medium gray suit with a pale gray shirt and no tie because he couldn't find it in his bag.

Chris passed the huge gorgeous arrangement of cut flowers she was holding to Pat to place on the altar in honor of their mother.

"They have a place reserved for them," she whispered to him.

Pat took the steps with haste and soon came back to escort the rest of them up the stairs and inside. Easter rode up on the exterior elevator. Each of them spoke to folks they knew, and Chris and Hallow hugged some old school friends who had come home as well. Most of the ladies in the church checked Pat from head to shoes, nodding, smiling, and whispering.

Once inside the sanctuary, Chris let her eyes adjust to the dimness and focus on the flowers sitting on an ivory cloth with *IN REMEMBRANCE OF ME* embroidered in gold thread. She caught a tear before it slid down her cheek. Her mother had sewn it and given it to the church some fifty years earlier. Even yellowed, she recognized it, still in mint condition otherwise. Mr. Gene, who had to be in his late nineties, slipped his arm around Chris and squeezed her tight. Chris had been the flower girl for his marriage to Mrs. Sophia, who sat near the front and waved at all of them when they walked by.

"Hey, Mr. Gene. How are you?"

"Fine," he grinned. "So good to have y'all home again."

"It's good to be here," Chris whispered as the siblings were ushered toward the front, smiling in amazement at all the colors and blooms the florist had arranged to perfection. They were too late to sit farther back, much to Easter's chagrin, and it was her fault. The family settled into the long pew, Easter suddenly coughing and covering her nostrils. A woman in the pew behind them wore enough perfume to gag a maggot. As they settled, the music started and the new pastor, Mark Stone, led the choir into the choir loft as he stepped to the pulpit to begin the service.

Easter nudged Hallow and grinned at her with a wink, letting her know she approved of the pastor's looks.

On the other side, Chris leaned over to Hallow and whispered, "I can't believe Mrs. Hazel still plays that organ every Sunday. She has to be in her late eighties."

"At *least*," Hallow said. "But she still plays well, doesn't she? She did a good job with Mama's funeral I thought." Even though she missed a few notes, the hymns she played were their mother's favorites. Everyone whispered or waved until the choir began singing.

After the offering plates were passed around, they all stood to bless the offering. Once the congregation sat, Mr. Stone came to the podium and announced that the flower arrangement was to honor Noel Holliday. He acknowledged the five children with a nod and then launched into his message.

Mark Stone, had been confirmed since their mother's funeral, and was a sixty-something with a head full of graying blond hair and a handsome but scruffy face who spoke articulately although their mother would not approve of the scruff. His dark glasses framed his face well.

"We have all heard the scripture:

Love is patient, love is kind. It does not envy, it does not boast, it is not proud. It does not dishonor others, it is not self-seeking, it is not easily angered, it keeps no record of wrongs. Love does not delight in evil but

rejoices with the truth. It always protects, always trusts, always hopes, always perseveres. 1 Corinthians 13:4-7.

"But let's take a closer look at what this passage reveals as ushers distribute the verse to each of you." He waited until everyone had a slip of paper to continue.

They took the small strip of paper, passed the plate on and settled in for the sermon, giving him their full attention.

"I'm certain that many of you have a job that is tremendously important to you, perhaps to the point of being revered by you." Pat squirmed. "Our jobs *are* important, particularly if we use them to serve others. But service is a message for another day. Today we focus on the fact that it doesn't matter what we do in life, what talents and gifts we possess if we don't have love. Without love, what we do amounts to nothing more than a hill of beans."

Chris could see some folks in the choir adjusting themselves in their seats and one man yawning. As tired as she was, she made an effort to stay focused.

The preacher adjusted his glasses and continued. "We must understand what love really is. Powerful love leads to action and, *yes*, sacrifice on behalf of others."

Hallow yawned and adjusted her hair, glancing over at Eve and Easter who seemed glued to the preacher's words. Love, at least the kind she'd experienced, had left her empty and hurt. Nevertheless, she tried to stay alert in case this man could offer her a different perspective in the next few minutes.

"Let's look at the passage **'love is patient'** for a moment. Patience involves a commitment of all one's soul, one's substance, if you will. All emotions, all will, and all thoughts. This is the kind of patience God gives us. I have to wonder where I would be if God weren't patient with me." He chuckled. "How about *you*? Where would *you* be without God's patience? He has to endure so much from us, doesn't he? We need to show this same kind of patience to others. Love, therefore, does nothing half-heartedly." He gave several examples of patient love.

Someone in the back started coughing but the pastor continued. "**'Love is kind.'** Let's talk about that next. Being kind involves much more than a friendly smile or greeting. Being kind involves giving people what they need, being honest, dependable, and serving. There's that word again," he smiled, looking over his glasses. The pastor told several stories where kindness exhibited great love for others.

His eyes locked on Eve's. At least she thought they were on her. She squirmed and blushed as he continued.

"This passage that I chose for today is called the 'Love Verse.' One can easily see why. This scripture contains every important teaching of God. Internalizing this passage can lead us to a more fulfilling life. That's why I had this particular scripture copied for each of you to take home with you. Read it daily and let it be your guide."

"The next part of this scripture is '**Love does not envy; it does not boast**." The pastor walked to the edge of the platform and glanced around. "I see some squirming out there." He gave examples of envy and boastfulness. His eyes then fell on Easter, and she could feel her face warm uncomfortably as he went back to the podium. She glanced at the strip of paper as he continued. "Envy and pride cause so much damage, folks. Both of these spring from self-centeredness. Envy is a result of wanting what other people have that we don't. Pride is a result of feeling that we're better than anyone else. Love makes no such consideration. God *is* love and love never fails! God's love and only God's love, living in us, can fulfill us. Can you *feel* it? Can you feel His presence in this place right now? If so, step out and come to the altar so that we can pray with you. Give your heart to Him who loves you in an awesome and powerful way!" He patted his heart. The choir stood and sang a closing hymn as several people worked their way to the end of a pew and went to stand with him as he prayed.

To Chris, the sermon which seemed to end abruptly was thought-provoking, and she enjoyed the old songs sung from a hymnal more than anything else. *Rock of Ages, Fairest Lord Jesus,* and *Amazing Grace* had always been some of her favorites, and even though the small choir made up of elderly folks struggled, she sang out to help them, the Spirit filling her soul and bringing tears to her eyes.

The pastor walked to the back of the sanctuary to speak to people as they left. Each of them shook his hand, and guests introduced themselves. He held on to Eve's hand a little longer than Chris thought necessary, but she did notice he wasn't wearing a wedding ring. Outside, the five Hollidays chatted with folks they knew before Easter and Chris climbed into Eve's Acadia to return to the house, Pat and Hallow deciding to walk the couple of blocks. They would eat lunch and change their clothes, figuring they had a full afternoon of work ahead of them.

The tiny town had only one restaurant and it was closed on Sundays, so the family spread the lunch they had organized over the phone. A bowl of chicken salad Chris had made came out of the fridge, and Eve set out the crackers she'd picked up to go with it. Pat fixed them all some sweet iced tea, and Chris and Hallow added seedless grapes, a jar of their mama's homemade pickles from the cabinet and some lettuce on which to place the salad. Easter set out napkins and paper plates.

"Eat up," Hallow said.

"Not until we bless this food," Chris quickly added. They held hands and bowed their heads while she said grace. Easter remained quiet throughout lunch.

"Easter, are you okay?" Chris asked after they had cleared the table and Hallow, Pat and Eve had drifted off to different places in the house.

She shrugged. "I'm not feeling too well right now. That's all."

"Anything I can do to help?"

"No, no, it's not physical, Chris."

"Then what is it?"

"I guess the preacher's sermon got to me. I mean," she turned to look Chris in the eyes. "He stepped all over my toes. He actually stomped my toes!" Easter's look was emphatic.

"What do you mean? About *love*?"

"The last part, the part about envy and pride. I have been so miserable for such a long time that during his sermon it was like God pointing fingers at me, you know? Like He's been so patient with me, and I haven't changed a bit. It's not God's fault I drove a car over one hundred miles an hour when I was a kid. It's not God's fault that I hurt all the time and stay unhappy and act so ugly." She touched Chris's arm. "Y'all don't deserve all the crap I've dished out. I'm so sorry, Chris.

I've harbored so much anger and turned it loose on other people, especially y'all."

"Oh, my goodness, honey," Chris wrapped herself around Easter and they hugged and shed a few tears.

"You, most of all, have shown me that kind of love, Chris. You've been so patient even when I know you wanted to smack me. And I deserved to be smacked. I've goaded you and the others for years when we were together. I barely have any good friends because I make them all miserable. Who wants a friend like *that*?"

"I love you, Easter. We all do, but I'm glad the message shook you up a little bit. You have so much to offer. If you can get past the bitterness or whatever you want to call it, you can make a great impact on other people, maybe others who have some sort of injury too. And I guarantee you'll find happiness."

"You're all going to see a difference in me," Easter told her oldest sister. "I promise." They hugged again and separated as Pat walked into the room.

"Anybody seen Hallow?"

"She took some things to her vehicle, I think," Chris said.

Pat nodded and headed for the door to have a private conversation with his sister.

24: HALLOW

I wasn't too upset that Pat knew about my circumstances and I felt better—relieved that he'd agreed to look into my financial situation. I had given him all the sordid details and as much information about Tricky Dicky as I knew. Pat had a good friend who was an attorney, he said, and with my permission, he would ask for assistance. He said they might involve a private detective, but I doubted anything would come of it. I really couldn't offer much help since Dicky used an alias and left no paper trail. I'd just have to start all over again. At least I knew I had the support I needed to move forward.

My mind drifted back to the men in my life, or at least the ones who'd stuck around for a while. Kent, my first husband, had been so busy building his career that he never had time for me. I was definitely not a priority. I'm not even sure I ranked in his Top Ten. Bob, my second mistake, smothered me, questioned my every move and made me more miserable than being alone had been. Mark, another significant error in judgment, was great in bed, but I soon learned what a deceitful, lying con man I'd married. However, Tricky Dicky outshone them all by ripping off everything I'd managed to accumulate in my adult life.

But my sweet brother reminded me that I still had my talent and determination, and I *could* start over again if I had to, even at my age. I smiled as I thought of Pat. Though he and I weren't particularly close, he was always there when I really needed him. And that mattered a great deal.

In my heyday, I'd made tons of money not just on Raleigh weddings but all over the state. My calendar stayed full nearly year-round. Brides and grooms often came to my beautiful home to plan, and I'd even had several small weddings there. But my heyday had passed as younger wedding planners emerged with fresh ideas on unexpected venues and floral designs. I still got a few smaller weddings of older couples who wanted a traditional second, third, or fourth wedding without all the expense and hoopla. Fortunately, I did have a social security check coming once a month. And the income continued after I'd closed my old bank accounts, opened new ones, and called all the important numbers to cancel credit cards and be issued new ones. I sighed and threw my head up.

"Stop punishing yourself, girl," I said aloud to myself. "Move on. Start over. You have a great professional reputation, and you can do this!" With that admission, I stomped the accelerator and ended the pity party in a better frame of mind.

25

Late May

The ocean was the roughest Chris had seen it since winter. Was there a storm she hadn't heard about or just strong wind offshore? She toed into well-worn sandals as her phone trilled.

"Hello?"

"Is this Chris Franklin?"

"Yes. Who's this?" Chris hadn't recognized the number on her cell phone.

"I'm Anne Morrison. I live next door to your sister, Eve."

"What's wrong?"

"Well, I heard her screaming and I went to find her. Her house—"

"I know it's a mess, Ms. Morrison," Chris admitted. *What an understatement.*

"Well, I had a time finding her. A loaded bookcase toppled over on her."

"Oh no! Is she okay?"

"No, I called my son to help me get the furniture off her. Then I called 9-1-1. Her ankle is twisted into a horrible position. I could see a bone sticking out. They took her by ambulance to the hospital in Rocky Mount. She asked me to call you."

Chris gulped down a sob. "I worried that something like this would happen."

"Well, it *has*," the neighbor said matter-of-factly. "I had no idea she lived in such squalor. She always seemed so nice and so neat."

"She *is* nice, Ms. Morrison."

"Oh, I didn't mean anything by that. Sorry. Well, I have to go."

"Thank you so much for calling me. And, please keep this between us."

Click ended the call. The whole town of Rocky Mount would know the situation in less than a day, Chris figured.

She dialed Hallow, who could get to Eve faster than the rest of them.

"Hey, Chris."

"Hallow, I need for you to get to the hospital in Rocky Mount. Eve has had an accident and you're closer than the rest of us."

"What happened?"

"It appears she broke her ankle," Chris explained, not wanting to get into details over the phone. "I understand it's a bad break. It's a long story, so we'll talk when I get there. I'll call the others. But can you go?"

"Yes, I just dressed for the day. I'll get a move on."

"Thank you. I'll get there as soon as I can."

After calling Pat and Easter, Chris packed an overnight bag and stopped to gas up before she left. The drive from Morehead City to Rocky Mount would take over two hours on a good day, and the sky looked as though it would open up and pour buckets at any minute. Hallow lived about an hour closer. Easter wanted her to pick her up, but Chris passed the buck to Pat, who would have to come after work if he could make it at all. His wife was flying in from Seattle and he hadn't seen her in months. Easter still didn't know about Eve's hoarding, but Hallow would soon find out. Chris felt an urgency to get to Hallow as well as to do what she could for Eve. She felt sure the neighbor would tell everyone she knew about Eve's hoarding and the outcome could be a devastating blow to her sister.

By the time Chris reached Kinston, the heavy rain had made it difficult to see the highway. Her cell phone rang. She clicked the Bluetooth button on her steering wheel when she recognized Hallow's number.

"Hallow?"

"Just want you to know I'm here and signed the papers for her surgery. I couldn't find her insurance card, but I know she's covered since she's a state employee. Her ankle is black and blue, swollen beyond belief, and painful. The ER doctor says it's broken in more than one place and he anticipates having to use metal screws to hold it in place. I don't understand how this happened, and she's medicated, so I'm not getting any information from her."

"Oh, no. That's bad. I'm in Kinston and about another hour away. I'll get there as soon as I can. I think I know what happened. I'm not sure if Pat and Easter will get there at all. Phyllis is flying in, and I hope Easter won't drive in this torrential rain by herself."

"It's stopped raining here. Slow down and be careful. Eve's going to be in surgery for a while and then in recovery. I packed a bag so I can stay overnight. We don't need the whole family here anyway. They would just be in the way. I'll try to find a phone number for Eve's school and let the principal know. She'll need a sub indefinitely, probably the rest of the school year."

"She sure will. Good idea to let them know as soon as possible. I packed a bag too. See you soon," Chris said, flipping off Bluetooth in her Toyota.

Eve had not come out of surgery when Chris met Hallow in the ER waiting room.

They hugged and Hallow began to pace. "Eve's been in surgery much longer than they said she'd be, and nobody has come to tell me anything." She grabbed Chris by the shoulders. "What if they had to amputate? Then we'll have two sisters who're handicapped."

"Don't even think that, Hallow. I'm sure this is extensive surgery and complicated. Many nerves run through the foot and ankle. It's delicate surgery. We want them to take their time and do it right," Chris explained.

"Well, you're the nurse, so I'll try to calm down. I still don't understand what happened inside her house to cause all this trauma. Once she's out, she'll be moved to a room and then we can go and sit with her. The doctor said he'd tell us what needs to take place when he can—probably a stint in rehab. And we've absolutely got to find her insurance card. They're hesitant to do much more without proof that she's insured."

"I'll tell you what little I know although it's going to shock the pants off you. Let's get something to drink from the cafeteria." They both got in the chai tea latte line and ordered the venti before sitting at a table.

"You said you might know what happened to Eve," Hallow said, hugging the paper cup in both hands.

"Yeah, and I just don't know where to begin, Hallow." Chris sighed deeply and looked her sister straight in the eyes. "I dropped by one day last month when I came up here for a DAR district meeting and knocked on the door. She didn't answer, so I went around to the back door when I saw her SUV out back. She'd locked the screen door, but I called out to her and she finally came to the door and told me to go away."

"Really? That doesn't sound like Eve."

"Well, the porch was loaded with stuff. Worthless yellowed newspapers in gigantic piles. Junk. All of it junk. I didn't know what to think, but I yanked on the screen door and it popped open, so I went to the main door and pushed it open." Chris stopped and reached for Hallow's hand. "She darted away when I shoved the door open. I mean I *had* to shove it open because it seemed blocked by something heavy."

"What was it?"

"Hallow, I've never seen a house like that in my life. Eve's a *hoarder*."

"No way!" Hallow's hand went to her chest and her mouth gaped open with shock.

"Yes, way. The house is piled high with junk in every single room. She hollered for me to leave, but I followed her voice deeper into the house, climbing over piles of newspapers, boxes and well, just junk. Scary stuff all the way to the ceiling in some rooms."

Hallow stared at Chris and didn't speak for a second. Then, glancing at her watch, she said, "We'd better get back, just in case the doctor's looking for us. I need to absorb this news slowly. We'll talk more later."

Chris nodded and together they headed up the hall.

According to the doctor, he put Eve's ankle back together with metal pins. She would stay in the hospital for a couple of days and then have to go to rehab for a few weeks at least. Chris decided that she and Hallow would approach the hoarding issue and, perhaps, try to clear the house before Eve was released. If that was even possible. She certainly couldn't move around and heal in that mess, and her insurance would only pay for twenty days in a rehab facility, so they had their work cut out for them.

Eve's pain medicine kept her loopy for several days so the sisters waited until she left the hospital to confront her.

The rehab center Eve would call home for a while was a state-of-the-art facility, clean and shiny, unlike the condition of Eve's home. Chris and Hallow held hands as they got to the #9 door, took deep breaths, and pushed the door open. Eve, propped up in the bed with her leg elevated gave them a weak look.

"Hey, girls."

"Well, aren't you the cheery one this morning?"

"The pain has eased at least for a while. This place is great," she said. "I ate the best breakfast I've had in a long time, and this really nice nurse gave me a bath," Eve said.

Hallow took a seat by the bed.

"I think the gown is gorgeous on you," Chris said with a nod.

"It's beautiful and so comfortable. Thank you for buying it for me. Most of my stuff at the house is well-worn."

"I'm sure," Chris said with a judgmental tone.

"Now don't start." Eve made an ugly face and Chris pulled up a chair. She and Hallow faced Eve, up close and personal.

"Eve, you *know* why this happened." It was not a question. Eve glanced at Hallow and then back at Chris.

"You told her, didn't you?"

"Of course! Eve, a huge bookcase loaded to the ceiling turned over on you! You could have been killed," Chris said in no uncertain terms.

Hallow reached over and grabbed Eve's hand which balled into a fist. "Calm down. We had to know. We *all* know, and we're going to help you."

Eve teared up, staring at Chris. "You promised not to tell!"

"I did no such thing. Anyway, when an over-filled bookcase fell on you, all bets were off."

"Pat and Easter know too?" The sisters nodded.

"What must you all think of me?" She burst into tears. Her sisters leaned in to hug her just as the nurse entered.

"What's wrong? What's going on here?"

"Oh, she's okay. Just upset. We're her sisters," Hallow told her.

"Mrs. Rockford, are you sure you're okay?" The nurse checked her pulse.

"Yes, I'm fine. My sisters are just being *sisters*," Eve attempted a smile.

"Okay, then. I'm just down the hall if you need me." She looked Chris and Hallow over as if they were cruel and left the door ajar on her way out.

"So, I guess we have a reputation here already," Hallow commented.

"I'm sorry if I upset you, Eve, but—"

"I know, I know. You love me and you're worried about me." Eve adjusted herself so that she could sit up straight. "Is this an intervention?"

"Yes," Hallow and Chris said at the same time.

"I know I can't go on living like I have been, but promise me you won't go over there and throw it all out." She looked from one sister to the other. "Promise!"

"Look, we want to help. We're your family, all four of us." Chris leaned in. "We know it's a disorder of some kind, but will you hear me out?"

A heavy sigh came from Eve's mouth. "Go ahead. I'm powerless to stop you at this point, but I assure you that if you cross me, I'll be vengeful," Eve told her emphatically.

"Okay," Chris pulled her chair a little closer. "Here's what we'd like to do with your permission: Hallow and I are both able to stay a few days and organize things at the house for you to go through later."

"Organize *how?*" Eve's face wore panic.

Hallow explained that they would buy up clear plastic bins everywhere they could think of and go to the house and gather like objects into those bins and label them, piling them in a safe place— maybe the garage— until Eve could sort through them.

"You can't possibly get all that stuff in bins," Eve said. "Besides, I want to do it myself."

"No, we can't get it all in bins, but it's a start," Chris admitted. "Will you allow us to do that much for you? Then you can just look at the bins and say 'save' or 'toss' when you go home."

"What's the catch?"

"Let us discard all the newspapers, trash, and empty boxes so it's easier to walk around in there. There needs to be a cleared path throughout the house, Eve."

"I don't know," Eve wrung the sheet between her hands, noticeably agitated.

"What good are the newspapers?" Chris's tone hit hard.

"They're …I…I save articles for school." Eve didn't look up at either of them.

"Wouldn't it make more sense to clip the article you want and throw the rest away? Besides, the ones I saw were yellowed and too brittle to use for anything." Chris paced the room. "And you probably won't be going back to school this year," she added.

Eve grabbed her head. "I have a headache. My foot is killing me. I can't do this right now." She pressed the button for her nurse and Chris and Hallow backed away.

"Do we have your permission to organize the bins and see if we can make some progress in that area?"

"I guess so," Eve said just as the nurse came through the door with pain medicine. "But where will you sleep?"

"Holiday Inn," Hallow announced quickly.

"Oh! We have to call Mr. Cannon, my principal," Eve suddenly called out.

"I already took care of it," Hallow said, reassuring her sister. "He said he or someone else from the school will touch base in a few days. I told him to go ahead and get a sub for at least two weeks, but it'll probably be a lot longer before you can get around on that ankle." Hallow glanced at Chris with a look that needed questioning later.

"Thank the good Lord I have plenty of leave saved up, and the school year's almost over," Eve replied in a whisper. "I think the pain medicine is kicking in." She sank back into her pillows.

"Wait! Where's your purse? We have to present your health insurance card to the hospital and this place."

"Um, I'm not sure. Try the bedroom," she said as her eyes fluttered and closed.

Her sisters kissed her cheek and silently headed down the hall. They would stop at a store and buy sterile masks and rubber gloves just in case they encountered disgusting things in the squalor.

After loading up on supplies at Walmart, the sisters checked into the Holiday Inn before heading to Eve's house in jeans and tennis shoes that covered their entire feet. Chris parked in back, and they entered the porch.

"Wow!" Hallow blurted. "This is worse than I thought it would be."

Putting the key in the back door and twisting it, Chris said, "You ain't seen nothing yet."

Hallow touched her sister's arm to stop her. "Chris, the principal said a lot more than I told Eve. He said he has to know by May first if she isn't planning on going back there because he needs to start hiring for next year."

"I figured that'd come up."

"But he also said he unlocked her supply room with his master key and he is . . . well, let me put it this way. *Furious* doesn't begin to cover it. He's having his custodians go in there and load it all up and take it wherever the school system dumps garbage."

"What? Surely there's useable stuff in there."

"No, he said apparently anything that had been put outside teachers' doors as trash, Eve carted off to her little hoarding room. Actually, a *big* room, he said. He asked me questions that I didn't know how to answer. I don't want the whole school talking about our sister as a nasty hoarder."

Chris blinked and said, "We're not even going to tell her about that, Hallow. Promise me!" Hallow promised, and Chris opened the door so they could climb over junk. Hallow tried to take it all in, muffling some expletives under her breath.

After Hallow saw the inside of the house, they made a plan to start by clearing the screened porch so they could then move things there, clear a room, and then do the same thing over and over until they could get to the floors and walls easily.

"But we promised not to throw things away, except for *real* trash," Hallow reminded Chris.

"Look for her purse first," Chris said.

"I know, but what is *real* trash? Mounds of old yellow newspapers, empty cardboard boxes, things that don't work, things that are broken?"

"All I know is that Eve will never speak to us again if we do this wrong, Hallow. She's fragile."

"Okay, I agree that we don't want to traumatize her, so let's fill up the yard trash cans first and go from there. I bought a box of those huge black yard bags and they can all be stuffed and hauled to the dump."

They stopped at a doorway, hauled themselves up on top of a piece of unidentified furniture. Then they held on to the top of the doorframe to enter the next room.

"How will we ever find her purse and get the insurance card in this *crap*?" Hallow's bellow filled the house with frustration. "Now, if I was a purse, where would I be?"

"Well, it's bound to be where she could find it and go to work or wherever and her keys to the house and car should be there too."

The sisters tossed bags, boxes, and other filth aside in search of the purse.

"Wait, is that her purse hanging on that hook over those pizza box piles?" Chris waded through the garbage to the kitchen counter near the back door and wrestled the purse off a nail. "At least we found it." She shook her head. "I'm taking it out to the car and locking it up with mine."

"Make sure her health insurance cards are in it before you do that, Hallow."

Hallow crawled over piles of paper boxes and rusty cans to get back to the door frame. Chris

watched her sister slide down into the next room
before she started back too.

Once Hallow returned, they began on the right
side of the porch, one holding a bag and the
other cramming it as full as possible before tying
it up and moving on. They managed to fill seven
lawn bags full, both professing it to be *real* trash.
They decided to leave those bags in the corner of
the porch until Eve gave them her consent to get
rid of them. At least by dark they could see the
gray-painted wood of the porch floor even though
it held many piles of what seemed to them
worthless junk. The tired sisters headed to the
hotel to shower and find something substantial
to eat.

Hallow found a TV channel that had soothing
sounds of ocean waves, and rested until her turn
to shower. When Chris exited the bathroom she
said, "Gosh, that sounds so good, like home. I
could go right off to sleep if I wasn't famished."

"Yeah, I've started sleeping with it on, and it
sure does help me." Hallow showered, and they
drove to the closest nice restaurant and ate until
they were stuffed. Back in the hotel, they each
climbed into a queen-sized bed and fell asleep to
relaxing beach sounds.

26: EVE

I'm not ready for an intervention. I tossed and turned so much in my hard bed that I hurt my foot, finally pushing my buzzer for some pain medicine in the middle of the night. Chris and Hallow were doing no-telling-what to my house while I was helpless to do anything about it. I had to get out of rehab! My belly flipped and flopped until I firmly placed both hands on it in hopes of calming down. I knew they were right, that after Matt died, I had turned inward to the point that our only child, Kirsten, had joined the military to get away from me. I lost myself somewhere along the way, thinking material things could replace him and fill the void left by both of them. But material things hadn't filled the void; they'd only filled the hours and the house to the rafters, literally. And I'd hardly even noticed.

Right after I finished my therapy, I grabbed my clothes and stumbled out the back door, barely keeping the crutches under me and hoping the alarm wouldn't go off and expose me during my escape. It didn't. I dialed a cab company and waited for it behind a big tree just in case someone stopped by the room to check on me. When the cab pulled up, the man got out and helped me into the back seat.

"You okay, miss?"

"Yes," I managed to eke out, although I wasn't okay at all. I gave him the address and we drove across town to my destination.

I heard Hallow say "This is a piece of garbage! In fact, *everything* in this room is garbage. Eve's a sick puppy."

"It's not all garbage to Eve," Chris responded. "And please don't let her hear you say she's sick, or Pat, and especially Easter."

Leaning on crutches, I felt my whole body tense up, stiffen even more, ready to pounce on them. My face felt hot with anger that I couldn't and wouldn't suppress.

"Ahem!"

They both turned and through their reddening faces under masks with eyes bulged, they said in unison, "Eve! What are you doing here?"

"I live here, in case you didn't *know* that," I huffed at them before tears streamed down my face. "What are y'all doing? You promised me you wouldn't take my things. These are my *things*! You have no right!"

Chris and Hallow tried to walk toward me, climbing and stepping and sinking into piles of upended furniture, lamps, and clothes that reached almost to the ceiling.

"Look at all this crap, Eve! It's trash, junk, garbage! Filth! It's got to go. Get over it!" Chris's voice was surprisingly loud and ugly and she stopped when she realized it.

I blinked, frozen in place, frozen from my oldest sister's blast. The one who always understood didn't understand at all. My sisters had ambushed me, outnumbered me while I was in a weakened state.

"Once you've buried the love of your life, you can feel free to tell me to get over it. Until then, Get. Off. My. Case!" I stared at Chris, watching her eyes suddenly fill with tears.

"Oh, Chris," my hand went over my mouth. "I'm sorry. I know you buried the love of your life. I'm so sorry. I shouldn't have said that." Chris nodded and turned away. Hallow stared at me.

The conversation had rapidly moved from heated argument to cold, awkward silence.

I wobbled a step and got one of my crutches caught. Blocked by everything around me, I looked down and then around. I suddenly realized stench came from every room in the house. As mad as I was with them, the sights and smells nearly gagged me. "I … I ah."

Why hadn't I noticed all this? Had I gone nose-blind? Had I really been living in this squalor? Roaches climbed out of boxes and mouse feces was on everything I could see. I retched.

"Stay still, Eve," Hallow called out with both hands towards me. "Don't move. Let me come to you." She slowly moved in my direction, struggling to step over piles.

"Hallow—"

"Just be quiet, Eve." Hallow's tone was sour and I said nothing more until I was safely on a stool.

"Y'all planned this behind my back after you promised me, and it is NOT going to happen!" I shrieked at them and stomped my crutch on the floor, although I knew it *was* going to happen even if they had to sedate me.

The door opened and Chris walked back in quietly. The two of them stared at me.

I looked around again and put my hand over my nose, trying to calm myself down. "I . . . I don't know what to say. I . . . had no idea it was *this* bad." I started to cry and shake, nearly crumbling before they reached me. Hallow slid the stool further under me just in time, and they hugged me even though they were both off-balance from the heap.

I made eye contact with them, and tears filled my eyes to overflowing. I sat there sobbing in hysteria, trying to take it all in. I had been eating, sleeping, and living in this filth. If you could even call it *living*.

"Eve, you have a problem," Hallow said softly.

"I don't have a problem! If *you* do, then get out of my house!"

Hallow and Chris just stared at me like I'd grown three monstrous heads.

"You can't be serious!" Hallow hollered at me.

"Stop it! Stop yelling at me!"

"Hallow, don't yell at her. Can't you see she's all to pieces?"

"You were yelling *too*, Chris."

"I . . . I know. I'm so sorry, Eve. We both need to be more sensitive. I guess we got caught up in the moment."

After I calmed a little, I admitted that something was missing inside me. Something in me had died along with Matt. But my sisters had butted into my private life more than I could tolerate. I just felt too weak to do anything about it at the moment. So I stayed quiet.

Finally, I said to my oldest sister, "Does grief lessen over time, Chris? I mean, can I *ever* get over him?"

"I suppose it does lessen a little. Yes, *yes,* it does," Chris added with emphasis. "Gradually. And sweet lasting memories take its place." She shuffled. "Henry is still present with me. Matt is still present for *you,* Eve. He's not something you 'get over.' You have to move forward *with* him. The special memories, the music you shared, the places that were favorites, the love you shared."

I turned wet eyes toward my oldest sister. "That's such a beautiful thought."

"It sure is," Hallow said, her own eyes filling up.

"We're here to support you, Eve. Honestly," Chris said softly.

"Yeah, sis. Let us help you." Hallow stayed quiet for a few minutes and then said, "Don't you want to unburden yourself? Make a clean break from all this crap?"

I felt my face screw up with renewed anger and frustration. "It's not crap to me. These are my collections."

"Collections? Seriously, girlfriend? Collections of rotted paper, nasty roach-filled smelly pizza boxes—"

"Hallow, stop," Chris called out.

"What I have and what I do with it is none of your business! It's nobody's business but mine!"

"Well, maybe we all need to leave. Lock the door and leave it all for you to deal with, Eve. We were trying to help, not make matters worse," Chris said softly.

I bit my lower lip. "Okay. Y'all are right. I know that." My voice was stressed and breathless. "I know you're right. I have to get rid of some things."

"*Some*?"

"Now, Hallow," Chris warned her sister.

"We know how much you loved Matt. Yes, he was a wonderful man, Eve, but do you think he would want you wallowing in self-pity? It's destroying you, honey. It's tearing you down little by little. You have to somehow rise above the grief and get on with your life. Matt would want that. Savor the many happy memories you had together and let them lift your spirit. That's the only way I've made it through Henry's battle with cancer and his death."

I couldn't utter a word, still full of guilt about my outburst.

Chris took a step back. "Okay, now. How did you get here?"

"I took a cab."

"The rehab center just let you leave?" Hallow furrowed her brows.

"Not exactly. I did rehab, and when they pushed me back to the room in the wheelchair, I got my crutches and clothes and snuck out," I confessed.

Both sisters put their hands on their hips.

"Well, Eve, you can't possibly think you can move around in this house on crutches. I mean, really," Hallow said.

I winced and wept more. They stayed close by and silent until I wore myself out. "I think my pain medicine has worn off." I felt limp, and my foot throbbed.

"We're loading you up and taking you back, Eve," Chris told me. They took off their gloves and lifted me off the stool.

I nodded and gave in . . . at least for the time being.

27: PAT

Even though Chris had filled me in on the situation with Eve, I had a more important mission to handle first. At RDU I waited an hour before the plane landed, pacing in the baggage claim area. I had to admit I was more nervous than I had ever been while waiting for my wife to return home. How does Phyllis feel about our marriage now, about coming back to me at this point? Has she remained faithful like I have? Does she want to stay married? Do I? I'd always thought that being married meant two people in love did things *together*. Our marriage had only been that way for a few years until she got a big promotion with a huge corporation that required traveling the world. My bank position had kept me in one place for forty years. She never wanted children since they would interfere with her career. I'd reluctantly agreed but now I wished I had a child, and perhaps grandchildren to spoil and enjoy as I get older.

On the other hand, a child would have kept Phyllis at home and probably unfulfilled, I supposed. Or the child would not have had the attention he or she deserved from either parent. I often worked late and usually ate a late supper out somewhere, not wanting to go home and cook in an empty house. And I do know how to cook. Mama had been patient with me when I wanted to be in the kitchen with her sometimes when my older sisters didn't especially want to or were too busy with their own lives. My two younger sisters could care less about cooking anything.

I let my mind wander until Phyllis rounded the corner. I waved, and her smile covered her whole face as she walked quickly to embrace me. A good start, I thought, a very good start.

Hallow saw her brother's name on her cell phone. "Pat?"

"Hey, sis. How are things going in Rocky Mount?"

"You wouldn't believe it, Pat. What a mess! Eve's got to have some help."

"Yeah, that's why I'm calling. I just can't come right now. I picked up Phyllis and we're back in Wilmington after going to the Angus Barn."

"Yum! That sounds divine. But I mean the kind of help a *troubled* person needs."

"Oh."

"Anyway, how's Phyllis doing?"

"Good. Tired, of course, coming in from Australia. She's soaking in the tub, so I thought I'd call and check on things. I tried Chris's number, but she didn't answer."

"Oh, she's in the shower. We're exhausted and have hardly made any progress. Eve has moved to rehab for a while, but she *did* give us permission to organize stuff into bins," Hallow told her brother.

"Well, from what Chris told me earlier, I'm surprised you can salvage anything."

"Only until Eve can go through it herself. She's emotionally fragile right now. She knows she needs help, but I guess she has to get over this broken ankle before she can deal with any of it." Hallow coughed. "We were scheduled to go back to Mama's house this weekend, but I don't see how we can do much except pick up the things we've already decided for each of us, or just leave it there until we can all go back."

"Yeah, about that. I don't need any of it. Maybe a few sentimental things, but I'm not arguing over it. Quite honestly, if I don't focus all my attention on Phyllis while she's home, she may stop coming home," he whispered into the phone. "That's just between us, Hallow."

"Really?"

"Yeah. Please don't say anything." Pat fumbled his phone. "I gotta go. Catch you later." Hallow heard the phone click in her ear just as Chris opened the bathroom door and stepped into the room in her robe.

"Who you talking to?"

"Pat. He and Phyllis are back in Wilmington,"

"Ah," Chris said, wrapping her head in a bath towel and patting it.

"Do you think they're okay?"

"What do you mean?"

"I mean their marriage, Chris. She's gone all the time. He's there alone. He seemed worried."

"I don't know. He and I have talked about it, and I *do* think he's concerned about how much she's gone." She fluffed her hair. "And yes, I do think he's lonely." She pulled on some jeans and a sweatshirt.

"Yeah, it's got to be a strain on their marriage," Hallow figured.

"But we can't fix it. They have to do that. So . . . I'm starved! Let's go get some food," Chris said.

"I'm with you, sis."

28

After a good night's sleep, Chris and Hallow dressed in casual clothes, grabbed their purses, and picked up a few items from the hotel's continental breakfast buffet on their way out.

"I'll drive," Hallow offered. Chris followed her to the white Acadia and they buckled up for the ride over to Eve's house.

"Maybe we can clear the kitchen today."

"I don't know, Hallow. Most of that stuff won't fit in bins," Chris pointed out.

"Most of it needs to go in the Dumpster," Hallow said. "but at least we can fill up some more trash bags and haul them to the porch so we can see the floor."

"Yeah, but at this point we can't even see counter-tops. I just don't understand how she could get so out of control," Chris said. When Hallow didn't respond, she continued. "I realize that something is mentally or emotionally wrong with Eve, but she's an intelligent woman, well-educated."

"It doesn't seem to matter how smart you are. I guess something just snapped in her after Matt died. He was a good guy. He looked healthy. I remember how shocked we all were when he died so suddenly."

"Maybe we should have made more of an effort to spend time with her after he died," Hallow eked out with a sad face.

"She's the one who insisted on going back to work so fast. And with me in Morehead City and you in Raleigh—"

"I know. Just trying to figure out when it all broke down, I guess." Hallow's head dropped in sadness.

They pulled into the back yard and parked behind Eve's old blue Acadia.

"Remind me to get a key from Eve and crank that thing once in a while," Hallow said while they got out of her vehicle.

They went onto the porch and opened the kitchen door, breathing a sigh of relief that nothing alive jumped out at them. They had locked their purses in the SUV and shoved cell phones into their pockets before donning rubber gloves and face masks.

"Let's see if we can get that book case up," Chris said. They struggled with the book case but, it was heavy and still loaded with books. "I guess we'll have to empty it to move it." Both sighed.

"Have you seen that hoarding show on television? The houses are worse than this and full of feces, dead or dying animals. It's just horrible to watch. And I never in a million years thought I'd be in one."

"I hope we don't run into anything nearly that bad, Hallow."

"Well, I'm going to be careful where I step and what I touch."

Hallow began pulling out bags for Chris to put trash in. First, the old rotting cardboard boxes and more newspapers went in. Some Chris had to gather in her hands because they were useless, yellowed thin puffs. Suddenly some kind of green cord entangled Chris and nearly tripped her.

"What's this?" She yanked on the cord until it flew into her face from under a pile of mess. "Looks like Christmas lights." She yanked some more and uncovered the top of an artificial tree leaning in the corner between the kitchen and the den. They both pulled on it, and once it was straightened up, tried to pull it out from under all the weight. It wouldn't come. "Something's weighing it down," Chris said.

"We're going to have to unload this corner to get to it." They crammed trash bags full of junk and dragged them to the porch, one corner of it now full. Hallow studied the porch. "We can't let all this stuff lean on the screen or it's going to pull out of the wood and end up out in the yard for possums and coons to get into. We'd better make sure they stand up. Let me find that long piece of twine I just saw and tie them to the hook up there." She pointed to the swing hook although they hadn't seen a swing.

Out of the corner of her eye, Chris saw the neighbor, Anne Morrison, walk around the end of the cedar trees and approach them.

"Good morning!" Chris called out. The neighbor didn't respond.

"Let me know if you need my son to help. He has a pickup."

"Oh, thank you, but we promised not to throw anything out until Eve looks at it," Hallow said.

"But it's worthless junk!"

"That's for Eve to decide," Chris countered with a sharp tone.

"Well, that's just sick!"

Chris turned her bag loose and walked toward the neighbor. "Yes, Eve is sick and she needs our understanding, not a lecture."

"Well, I hope she gets some help *soon*." With that comment, the neighbor huffed and quickly went back to her side of the hedge.

"Boy, that woman's a total—"

"Yes, she is," Chris interrupted.

"You know, I've been thinking about this situation. Eve can't see through these black bags. And it's all truly trash. She probably wouldn't even notice if we hauled them off. Then she could walk around and look inside the clear bins in each room."

"I know you're right, Hallow, but we promised," Chris emphasized, stopping in her tracks, suddenly weak in the knees, and her hands didn't want to grasp anymore.

"What's wrong, Chris?"

"Oh, just a moment of weakness, I guess. But my hands hurt." She looked down at them, swollen, stiff, and red.

"Gosh, did something bite you?"

"I wouldn't be that surprised." Chris headed out the door to get a cold bottle of water from the cooler they'd brought. She guzzled it down and her energy returned.

"You know what, Chris? I just remembered that animal shelters are always in need of newspapers for the cages. Maybe we should fill some of the better boxes with intact papers and take to them," Hallow suggested. "It's only a few miles from here."

"That's a great idea. But we need to find a place to put them in the meantime."

By noon they had managed to get the Christmas tree on the porch with its lights still dangling here and there. Most of the tree had been crushed under the weight of other things and they decided it was not worth saving.

"I'm thinking that we're going to have to haul some of if off because we're already running out of porch and we haven't even seen the kitchen floor yet. We need more help, Chris."

"Yes, we do. And I'm also thinking that you're right about Eve having no idea what's under all the stuff that's on top. Maybe we can get some help to haul off the trash bags, at least. This would be too overwhelming for her to deal with anyway. I'll walk over and ask the boy to haul these away.

"I'm with you, sis. Maybe he can stand the bookcase up for us too."

Chris soon came around the hedge with her hands beating the sides of her thighs. Hallow turned to her. "Well?"

"Ha! He wants ten dollars a bag. That would be seventy dollars now and hundreds more to come. I told him 'no thanks'."

"Well, we'll just pile them in the corner until Pat can come with his truck," Hallow said.

"Yeah, I guess that's the best thing to do. Should have known help wouldn't be free," Chris said, glancing back at the neighbor's house and entering the porch again. "Let's go get some food. I'm tired, ill as a snake, and my tummy's growling."

"Sounds good to me." Hallow checked her watch. "Wow, it's already two o'clock. No wonder we're hungry."

29: EASTER

I felt left out, one more time. My sisters were in Rocky Mount trying to help Eve, and Pat had picked up his wife and wanted to lavish lots of attention on her while she was home. So, that left me on my own again. I threw a dish towel across the edge of the sink and opened the refrigerator door, using my cane to get to the table to feed my face. What few friends or acquaintances I had were all busy having a life.

Even though Chris had called and told me about Eve's situation, I was disgruntled because my bossy oldest sister had told me in no uncertain terms not to come up there unless it was only to see Eve at rehab. She'd made it clear that she didn't want me to go to Eve's house. Well, Chris wasn't my boss. I'd go if I wanted to. I poured coffee and snatched at my toast with my teeth, making the decision to pack a bag and drive north.

30

After eating cold fast food, the sisters called Eve and found out Easter had come to Rocky Mount.

"Good grief! I told her not to come," Chris said to Hallow. "I just hope she gets in a nice long visit and then heads on home."

"I wouldn't be surprised if she showed up at the house. Let's hope not, though."

"She couldn't begin to walk in there. We're hardly getting around ourselves," Chris added. "But you're probably right. She never pays any attention to what I say."

They got back to work filling trash bags until they ran out. They were dragging them to the porch to wedge against a wall when their youngest sister pulled into the driveway.

"Told you," Hallow said. Chris shook her head.

"Oh no! Easter, don't even get out," Chris yelled, heading to the VW. "You can't possibly walk in that house."

"I just want to see how bad it really is," Easter replied.

"Our sister is a hoarder. What else do you need to know?" Hallow put her hands on her hips and blocked the porch door.

"What's in all those bags?"

"Trash," came the response in unison.

"Nothing but trash. We promised Eve we wouldn't throw anything else away, but the amount of trash is unimaginable," Chris told her.

"Well, I'm to report back to Eve on what you're doing, so step aside and let me look," Easter said, pointing her cane at Hallow.

"Fine. Have it *your* way." Hallow moved aside and let Easter get up the steps the best way she could and peek into the kitchen.

"Goodness! This *is* bad. I see what you mean. I can't walk in there."

"We haven't even touched the rest of the house. We're just trying to work our way one room at a time. Today is Day Two," Chris explained.

"I've seen some of those shows on television but I've never seen anything like this in person," Easter admitted. "What can I do to help?"

"I don't know of anything you can do until she gets out of rehab. She certainly can't come back and live in this, and I doubt any therapists would want to come here either."

"Well, a doctor came by and told her she could go home Friday."

"*What?*" Hallow looked stunned.

"No way she's coming *here*," Chris called out from a kitchen corner.

"So, where does she go then if you're both here going through this mess?" Easter used her cane to make a circle.

Chris and Hallow stopped working and came out on the back steps with Easter. "Well, if you *really* want to help, take her home with *you*," Chris said.

"What? Don't be ridiculous! I can't take care of her. I can barely take care of *myself*."

"Yes, but she'll have a walker, and your place is handicap accessible, isn't it?" Chris pushed forward.

"Yeah, but it's tiny. Two small bedrooms and one bathroom. Besides, her doctor's up here."

"She can be recommended to a doctor in Jacksonville, have rehab there, and stay with you until a better option comes up," Chris added. "At least you have two bedrooms."

Easter glared.

"I'm merely making a suggestion. You *said* you wanted to help." Chris stumbled at bit, light-headed.

Easter turned to Hallow. "Why aren't you saying anything?"

Hallow shrugged. "Chris has a point. I live in Raleigh and she lives in Morehead City. Neither of us is at home until we get this situation under control. Pat's in Wilmington working and trying to spend some time with Phyllis. You're the only family member who can do it, Easter."

"What about Kirsten? She's Eve's daughter. Wouldn't they allow her to come home and take care of her mother?"

"Kirsten is in Germany, Easter. I doubt that a broken ankle would be considered an emergency to the army," Chris explained, perching on the corner of a chair to get her breath.

Easter sighed heavily as she headed to her Beetle. "I'll have to think about it."

"You have until Friday," Chris said looking her dead in the eyes. "Otherwise I guess we'll have to find her another place to live or a hotel that'll eat up her pay check in a hurry," Chris reminded.

"Not to mention if her leave runs out, her days missed at school will come out of her paycheck," Hallow said.

"Doesn't she have enough years in to retire? Surely she does." Easter looked hopeful.

"I think so. She just doesn't know what to do with herself."

"Well, let me go home and see if there's any way to rearrange my apartment for two crippled folks. If I think it'll work, I'll call Eve and see if she'll agree to come. But only until she can make it on her own again."

"That would be great, Easter," Chris said. "Please try. Anything would be better than her being alone right now. She's more fragile than I ever realized."

They watched Easter drive away, and Hallow turned to Chris, who was frantically scratching her ankles.

"Are you okay?"

"I don't know. My hands feel better, but now my ankles are driving me nuts." She lifted her jeans and saw red splotches around her right ankle bone and on her left front leg. "Maybe there's something in my socks." She pulled off her shoes and socks, shook them, peered inside them, and found nothing. She had an idea what it might be, but she wasn't ready to tell Hallow, or anyone else for that matter.

They headed back into the house and Chris uncovered several small rusted metal tables large enough for a snack and a drink and pulled them to one side. She then grabbed a folding lawn chair with the bottom nearly shredded. Worthless. She decided to put it on top of a trash bag.

"How are you coming along in the kitchen, Hallow?"

"Well, I've found two nice ceramic bowls but they're huge. I can't imagine what Eve put in them," she called through the window. "They're in good shape, so we need to find a spot to put things that we're saving."

"Yeah, I guess since the weather's nice, we could pull out some sheets and make a SAVE pile, DONATE pile, and TRASH pile like they do on those shows."

"That sounds good in theory, Hallow, but since we promised not to make those decisions for Eve, we can't just put stuff outside and leave it there. We'd end up moving it all twice."

"True."

"At least we can see each other now," Chris said. "Oh, here's a nasty window fan. I guess she used this in the spring and the fall, but it's filthy. I'll plug it in when I find an outlet and if it doesn't work, it's going in the trash."

"Ouch!"

Chris peered through the window. "What's wrong?"

"I just cut my hand on some broken glass," Hallow said, throwing a few things to the side.

"I'll come and help you."

Together they pulled out broken pottery and a picture frame with large shards of glass. "We need to bandage that, Hallow or you could end up with a nasty infection from all this crap. There's no telling what all's in here. We probably need tetanus shots."

Hallow agreed and since they were both exhausted, they locked the house and headed for the hotel, stopping at a drug store to pick up peroxide and something to wrap the cut. "I'll need more gloves. That sucker cut right through this one," Hallow pointed out.

After disinfecting Hallow's hand, they went down the street to a pizza joint and ate a large one together with small side salads. Chris called a local animal shelter. Their outgoing message said they would take newspapers and old towels and could use old spatulas and slotted spoons for the cats. She made a note to save those items or at least those in good enough shape to be useful. As soon as they returned to the hotel, they took turns soaking in a tub filled with bubbles, hopped into their beds and turned out the light on another tiring day.

Day Three was going more smoothly because they started putting empty boxes and cloth bags in the musty garage—dark and seemingly full of racks of clothing they would deal with later. They loaded newspapers strong enough to hold urine, ragged kitchen towels and tools for the shelter into a large canvas bag they'd found. They could now see most of the kitchen and decided to leave it to Eve to go through the rest whenever she could. They moved on to the den and filled five more trash bags and hauled another large pile of newspapers and magazines to the damp and musty garage.

"I'm not saving any magazines. Some of these issues are at least three years old. I swear I want to strangle her!" Hallow shouted out in anger. "I've lost all the beautiful expensive things I had and she hoards trash! I—" She stopped talking when she looked up at Chris who let the hands on her hips speak for her.

"She's sick, Hallow. It's a disorder."

"I know, but it still makes me mad."

"I know you're angry, but don't take it out on Eve. Be mad at that horrible beast you let into your own home." Chris's voice had risen too. "By the way, what are you going to do about that?"

"Pat is consulting a lawyer friend of his on my behalf. I think he's dealt with this sort of thing before, but I don't see how he can help. I don't even know what the butthole's name was."

"Are you going to sell the house?"

"I may not have a choice. I can't live on just social security."

"What about the weddings you planned? Surely they pay well."

"They are far and few between, Chris," Hallow confessed. "Younger planners are getting most of the gigs I once got. I guess I'm considered too traditional for the younger generation."

"Look, you have to get back in the game. Come up with something that sets you apart from the others but is traditional and classic. Be unique. You've always been so good at wedding planning. You've always been empowering, Hallow and I've always admired that."

"You have?"

"Yes, I have." Chris grabbed Hallow by the shoulders and pulled them up straight. "Now put on your big girl panties, pull yourself together, and get control of your life again." Hallow stared at her. "Sermon is over. Go forth and do good." Hallow smiled at her sister and hugged her, wiping away a stray tear.

They turned back to the job at hand, remaining silent for a while in the garage.

"Look, I've found a jewelry armoire."

"Pull it out, Hallow." They both tugged the chest out of a tight web of trash and found a space flat enough to put it down and open it.

Chris's mouth flew open. Even though Eve seldom wore much jewelry, she had at least a dozen pearl necklaces, all similar.

"Do you suppose she hit a big sale? Or maybe planned to gift them?"

"Not hidden in this mess, Hallow. Just more hoarding, I imagine," Chris said.

Earrings, some broken, lay in disarray, strewn with no reasonable way to pair them for wearing. Suit pins, beautiful broaches were in odd places, not protected at all.

"Wait!" Chris called out. "That's one of my favorites and it belongs ... belonged to Mama! What's it doing in Eve's jewelry box?"

"Um, I don't suppose they could just be similar?"

"No, Hallow. This is *Mama's*. I'm sure of it," Chris stood and started looking around. "Look over there, Hallow. Those are Mama's scarves."

"They sure are." Hallow walked over and picked up a few. "And they stink too. And here's a purse that I'm almost sure was Mama's. We all promised not to take anything out of the old house without permission."

"Do you think Mama gave her all this stuff? Or did Eve just help herself to them?" Chris clenched her teeth and felt her blood pressure try to strangle her. They both knew the answer to that question.

"Calm down, Chris, before you have a heart attack," Hallow said touching her sister's arm. "We'll get to the bottom of this later." She sniffed the air and coughed. "And have you noticed how awful it smells in here?"

"Yeah, I'm coughing and my head is clogging up." Hallow found an overhead light and flipped it on. They went over to some clothes racks, filled with musty clothes from all four seasons. Chris pulled a leather coat from the rack near her. "Oh my gosh! It's covered with mold, Hallow!" She dropped it on the concrete.

"I'll bet that coat cost her a pretty penny, too."

They began looking around at the entire garage. "This place is full of mold and mildew. Even all the shoes are covered and these purses. Let's get out of here!"

They walked back into the main house and locked the garage door behind them, not believing that it had taken so long to realize the hazardous air they'd been breathing.

"It's all got to go," Chris said. "I don't care how much she paid for all this stuff. It simply has to go!"

Hallow nodded agreement.

31: CHRIS

The plan was to check on Eve the following morning, and Hallow and I would go to our own homes to take care of personal business and rest for a few days before tackling Eve's house again. And the mold and mildew issue would have to be discussed and taken care of by professionals. I had no business in that house while it was filled with mold. Neither did Hallow for that matter.

I had good days and bad days, limping when my joints cried out in pain. I'd been diagnosed with psoriasis several years back, and the doctor warned me that it could turn into PsA, psoriatic arthritis, like the golfer, Phil Mickelson, had. I hoped it wouldn't get bad enough to take shots because, as a former nurse, I knew how many adverse side effects most biologics had. Yet here

I was, most of my hidden body parts covered with itchy scaly plagues that tormented me and more joint pain than I'd ever had in my life. My energy level came and went—in a hurry—at odd times. With all the cleaning up at Eve's and at the old home place, I'd tried to hide my discomfort from Hallow, but my sister had figured out something was amiss. All of my siblings counted on me to be the strong one. Now I wondered how soon I'd need them to help me. For now, though, I would continue to tough it out and get Eve's situation under control, one way or another.

32

The following morning, they checked out of the hotel and went to the rehab facility where Eve had progressed enough to be released. Much to their surprise, Easter was already there.

"They're releasing her," she told them in the doorway. "I'm taking her home with me, at least for a few days. She's worked really hard."

"That's wonderful, Easter. Thank you for doing that, but I'm surprised Eve will go."

"Somewhat begrudgingly, but what choice does she have? I can't do what y'all are dealing with, but I can take her to a nice clean house that's handicap-accessible. I told her we'd take her SUV and leave my Beetle at her house. Hopefully it'll be okay there in the yard. Dr. Chadwick arranged for PT to come to my place because of *my* condition, so that'll help both of us."

"It sure will. We locked up the house but she can peek in the windows and see some of her kitchen now," Chris said. "Hallow and I both need to do some things at our own places and then we'll come back. Pat said he'd try to help us. Maybe Phyllis too."

"Good. It'll take all the hands you can find to clean up that mess," Easter whispered, looking back to make sure Eve hadn't heard her.

"Look, we need to have a serious conversation with her. You need to hear it too."

"Okay. At least she's in good spirits this morning," Easter said.

Hallow and Chris glanced at each other, knowing they were about to change Eve's spirit. After a few pleasantries were exchanged, they all sat down around the unmade bed to inform her of the dangerous mold situation. Eve didn't want to hear any of it, placing her hands over her ears.

"Eve, if the city finds out, they're going to condemn that house." She stared at Chris. "Seriously, they will, honey. It's not only full of things," Chris said as delicately as she could manage, "but it also has rodents, insects, and mold. The mold is thick and dangerous. It's all over the clothes in the garage."

"I'll get to it. I just have to heal, and then I'll go through everything, I promise. Just don't rush me. And don't *report* me," she added with sadness.

"We wouldn't do that to you, Eve, but your neighbor might. She isn't a nice person," Hallow told her.

"That snotwad? This is none of her business!"

"True, but she saw it all when you screamed for help. Remember? She called the rescue squad and then called me," Chris reminded her sister.

Eve's head dropped.

Hallow stood up and clapped her hands. "We need to make this fun, you know?" They all stared at her.

"*Fun?* When did you donate your brain, Hallow?" Easter glared at her sister.

"Well, maybe fun is the wrong word. You know what a challenge this is going to be. We—Chris and I, maybe Pat—can pull things out on a pretty day in piles to donate, save or throw away, Eve. Then the saved stuff can be moved to a storage facility, donations taken to Salvation Army, and trash can be discarded. Kinda like a puzzle."

Chris rose. "That's not a bad idea. And then Easter can bring you from Jacksonville to go through what's in the yard. It'd be so much easier on you that way. And maybe, just maybe, Pat can arrange to help us. Phyllis, too. Then we can lock up and do the same the next weekend," Chris said in a chipper voice.

"No," Eve suddenly vocalized. "No way!"

Chris reached for her sister's trembling hand. "Look at me. Look. At. Me!" Eve's eyes came up to meet hers, with tears flooding them. "You're going to end up losing *all* of it if you don't let us help you. If the city inspector sees it, you might not even have a chance to save the *good* things. Please, I beg you, let us do this."

"We're doing this with or without your approval, Eve," Hallow blurted out, looking over Chris's shoulder.

Eve glanced at Easter for support.

Easter shrugged. "You might as well suck it up, cupcake. It looks like it's going to happen."

In a tired weak voice, Chris said, "Go home with Easter and let Hallow and I do this. We'll get it to a point where you can come back and make decisions easier."

"Come on, Eve, let's go." Easter headed for the door.

"I'll take your bag," Hallow said.

Eve rose slowly, conceding defeat, and got into the wheelchair so Chris could push her to the SUV.

Chris and Hallow left, hoping Eve could pull herself together, find someone to deal with the mold, and cope just fine at Easter's house. She seemed in a better frame of mind, and that would help. Hallow headed west to Raleigh and Chris aimed her Highlander towards Morehead City, looking forward to getting home for a few days of rest with no drama.

33

Easter texted that she and Eve would stop at the house for a quick look and then travel on to Jacksonville. They all texted a thumbs up icon.

Chris's phone rang at 12:43, and it was Easter's cell.

"Where is all my stuff?" Eve's voice blared through the phone.

"What do you mean?"

"You *promised* not to take anything away until I could go through it," Eve shouted at her.

"We didn't. We just piled all those big trash bags on the porch but they really *are* trash, Eve."

"There's nothing on the porch but two metal tables," she responded.

"What? They were there when Hallow and I left," Chris assured her sister as her phone beeped that she had another call. "Can I call you right back, honey? Pat's calling me." The phone clicked in her ear, and she slid her phone to answer the other call.

"Hey, Pat."

"Hey, sis. Where are ya'll?"

"I'm on the way home, Hallow's headed back to Raleigh and Easter is taking Eve to Jacksonville."

"Well, Phyllis and I got up real early this morning and drove to Rocky Mount, thinking we'd see everybody. We went to the house and I hauled off all the trash on the porch. I couldn't get inside, so that's all I could do. By the time we got to the rehab place, Eve had checked out," he explained.

"Oh, *that's* what happened," Chris said. "I wish you'd called me before you did that. I just got a call from Eve. She's hysterical that the trash got hauled off before she went through it."

"I'll call her then. I didn't mean to start trouble."

"I know. It really *is* trash, Pat. But Eve needed to trust us. We'd promised not to move it until she could go through it. Did you look in the windows?"

"Yeah, I couldn't see much because it was so dark in there, but enough to know what a mess it is. I'll call Eve and apologize."

"You can expect to be blown out. And, Pat, she's so fragile, embarrassed, and feeling rotten. Be gentle."

"Okay. By the way, Phyllis says, 'hi'."

"Tell her 'hello' as well. We need to get some people to help before the city condemns the place. There's a lot of mold in the garage and probably all over the house."

"Phyllis and I can help," Pat offered, "but you'll have to hire a pro for the mold."

"It would be nice to have your help. I don't know if Eve will hire a pro, but I'm leaving that decision to her even though her options are getting fewer by the day. If the city finds out about it, they may condemn the place and she won't be able to get even the good stuff out, if there *is* any good stuff."

"Well, we'll head back to Wilmington if there's nothing we can do right now. I guess we could go back a different route and stop by Easter's on the way home," he added.

"I don't know, Pat. I'm sure Eve will be tired by the time they get there, and she's emotional right now. Hallow and I are both physically worn out."

"Has Eve got enough time in to retire?"

"I think so, or at least she's pretty close and probably has enough leave to make it total thirty years."

"Well, maybe she'll consider doing that." After a long pause, Pat said, "I guess we'll go on home then. Catch you later."

Chris clicked off without saying anything else. She didn't care if that was rude. She'd about had enough of being the oldest and most responsible one in the family. As much as she loved her brother, she could no longer hide the fact she was miffed that he hadn't called one of them before deciding to dump the trash and make matters more difficult. He *could* have called. He *should* have called. He had all their numbers. The only strong male in the family got up every morning and went to his pristine office at the bank and had normal desk hours while she and Hallow had about killed themselves dealing with the mess Eve had made. He *should* have called and taken more responsibility rather than leaving it for her, as usual. She reached for her forehead, the pain from a stress headache taking its toll and making her more resentful of her brother and feeling guilty about it at the same time. She looked up and said, "I'm sorry, God. I know I disappoint you. Please give me strength and fill me with loving thoughts for my siblings."

34

June

The Rocky Mount Sanitation Department number showed up on Eve's cell phone. Eve froze in place.

"What's wrong, Eve? You look like you've seen a ghost," Easter said. Eve turned the phone toward her sister.

"You answer it."

"Uh, um, okay. What am I supposed to say?"

"How should I know?" Eve's voice was loud and stressed. Easter waved a hand and mashed **Accept.**

"Hello?"

"Mrs. Rockford? Mrs. Eve Rockford?"

"No, this is her sister. What can I do for you?"

The man cleared his throat. "I'm Jim Townsend, an inspector for the city of Rocky

Mount. I need to speak to Eve Rockford, who owns the property at 1602 Francis Street."

"She is indisposed right now. She asked me to answer the phone," Easter said emphatically.

"Okay. Are you aware of the situation inside her house, ma'am?"

"What situation?"

"I, um, this is a delicate matter, ma'am. Please have Mrs. Rockford call me, Jim Townsend." He rattled off his phone number.

"She has caller ID," Easter said, cutting off his words.

"Okay, then I will expect to hear from her before the day ends." Easter heard a click.

Eve was in her face. "Well?"

"He wouldn't tell me anything. He says it's a delicate matter, and you have to call him before the day's over."

"Or what?"

Eve defiantly waited a week to call Jim Townsend. He told her that a neighbor of hers called in that her house was 'uninhabitable', and he needed to go inside and inspect it before filing his written report to the city. She told him she currently lived with her sister in Jacksonville and not in the house, but he insisted that they make an appointment. Reluctantly Eve set a date and time to meet. Since she wasn't yet driving, Easter would take her and then disappear until Eve called her to pick her up.

The man with a rugged complexion and a head full of curly dark hair with gray tips walked around the house perimeter. They had noticed the white city-issued truck parked in the driveway.

"Are you sure you want to do this alone, Eve? I can stay if you want me to," Easter offered.

"It'll be fine, Easter. You can't get around in there anyway, and I'm hoping this will be quick." She brushed her sister's arm. "Wish me luck."

"Fingers crossed."

Having graduated from the crutches, Eve stepped out using her cane for support and toddled toward the man.

"Mr. Townsend?" She forced a smile. "I'm Eve Rockford."

He shifted his iPad and threw out his hand. "Nice to meet you, Mrs. Rockford." He was tall and almost too thin. She shook his hand reluctantly.

"I've walked around the property and outside is not too bad. Just minor. But I need to go *inside*. We can do this the easy way, or I can get a search warrant."

"You make me sound like a criminal, Mr. Townsend. A warrant isn't necessary, but this is all so embarrassing. I can't believe my neighbor called my house a problem."

"Well, she *did* say she and her son had to dig you out from under a bookcase, Mrs. Rockford. That sounds like a serious problem and definitely got our attention." He looked down at her ankle.

Eve's face turned red and his iPad made her more nervous. He was going to take notes! She waddled her way up onto the porch and reached behind a shutter to get the extra key.

"Well, let's get this over with then," she said with a sharp tone.

She moved to the side and gestured for the inspector to go inside. After he entered, taking in the scene methodically, she went in and sat on the kitchen stool to watch his reaction. He typed notes on his iPad and climbed over mounds of stuff into other rooms. He seemed to be gone a long time but once he came into view, Eve could see a worried look on the man's face.

"I want to help you, Mrs. Rockford, but this is a serious problem."

"How? I mean, what do you propose to do to help me?"

"I'm a code enforcement officer. Your hoarding and accident present a clear danger. You have to clean this place up, or the city is going to condemn it not only because it's dangerous but that mold is even worse. You'll be homeless if I condemn it, Mrs. Rockford. I have to advise you to get rid of all this clutter, clean up the unsanitary conditions, and remove the mold hazard."

Eve wobbled to the porch, sat on the top step, put her head in her hands and sobbed. "I don't know what to do." She whimpered for a few minutes while Jim Townsend stood by.

After several minutes he said, "Let's start with getting all the trash out of here and setting things upright. You can't have any furniture falling on you again. You were lucky you weren't hurt much worse." He gave her time to process what he'd said and then added, "Then you'll have to make some tough decisions."

Eve looked into his dark brown eyes and said, "Okay." He smiled weakly at her and offered a hand for her to stand. She took it and came up to meet his eyes again.

"How's the ankle?"

As she caned her way back up the steps with his help, she replied," I'm getting there, but it's been a slow process."

"I imagine the ankle is a difficult place to heal," Jim said.

"That's what they tell me although I've been diligent with therapy mostly because my sister, Easter, is a slave driver and she has a personal trainer. Between the two of them, I'm rocking and rolling," Eve said with a lighter lilt in her voice.

"Well, as long as you're rocking just a little on that cane and not rolling on the floor," Jim responded with a wink. Eve turned to the side with her cane as support.

"Thank you for offering to help, Mr. Townsend. My sisters have tried, but none of them live here, and I think they're all overwhelmed with this mess. Quite frankly, I am too, in addition to being in emotional as well as physical pain."

Jim nodded. "Okay. Let's come up with a viable plan. I think it's best if you only supervise until we can get some cleared paths throughout the house. How about I grab some lawn bags and gather up the empty boxes and stuff we know is real trash. Once things are uncovered, you can make decisions."

"You sound as if you've done this before."

"No, I haven't, but it kind of seems like the only way to start, you know?"

"I guess so." Eve hung her head in shame. "I never intended for this to happen, Mr. Townsend."

"I just want to help you put all this in perspective. I'm certainly not experienced, but I have heard others talk about how they confronted something like this. And please call me Jim."

"Eve," she said softly.

He touched her wrist. "Eve, I'm not here to judge you. In fact, I'm only supposed to look around and turn in a report to the city. Since you don't have any help and you're injured, I'll help you. You can run me off at any time." His smile seemed genuine.

"You're a God send," she said. "Thank you."

"Well, I don't know about that, but the city sure sent me." He managed a quick laugh. "Okay," he whirled around and started stuffing boxes, bags, paper plates, cups, and plasticware into a large bag.

"Make sure there's nothing in those boxes!"

Eve texted Easter and told her to go shopping or find something to do since the inspector had offered to stay and help for a while.

Easter texted,
I'll get mani/pedi

"Yes ma'am. Checking all of them," he assured her, glancing back at where she perched.

After two hours of stuffing trash into bags and hauling them out to his truck for disposal, Jim pulled a stool up next to Eve again.

"How are you holding out?"

"I can't believe how tired I am just watching you work," Eve managed a weak response.

"I imagine it's more emotional stress than tiredness, and you're still healing." He looked down at her ankle. "And that bad boy is swollen. What if we stop and go somewhere for a burger where you can prop it up on a booth?"

"Sounds like a plan, but I need to call my sister. Maybe she can join us." He lifted her and helped her wobble down the porch steps and over to his truck.

"I've got a running board on here, but I may have to kinda lift you up anyway," Jim said.

"It's okay. I won't think you're being fresh," Eve smirked at him. They both laughed.

"Good. I don't want to be fresh."

Eve texted Easter, but she declined to join them for lunch. Jim drove to Wendy's and Eve worked her way into a booth and slid back enough to put her ankle on the seat. Jim ordered and sat on the other side. As they ate, both studied each other, trying not to be too obvious.

After a while, Jim leaned in. "So, tell me, how did such a beautiful lady get into such a mess?"

Eve looked around at the crowd in the restaurant, raking her teeth across her bottom lip. "Perhaps another time and place." Her face appeared stunned as her voice broke. She took her last bite of burger and popped the last fry in her mouth, put her legs down and started sliding to the end of the booth.

Jim stood. "I'm sorry. I didn't mean to upset you."

He offered his hand to help her up. "I can manage by myself," she snapped, teetering for a second before she found her balance.

They drove back to her house in silence. Once there, she opened the door and put her cane on the ground. "Thank you for lunch."

"I thought I'd help all day," he explained. He jumped out of his truck and ran around to her side.

"No," Eve snapped again. "I can do it myself."

"Eve, look, I . . .I didn't mean to upset you. I'm not here to judge you. I just want to help." He spread his arms and looked at her pleadingly.

"It's not your responsibility. It's *mine*. All mine. I made the mess and I'll get it cleaned up." She avoided looking him in the eye.

"But you're still using a cane. You can't possibly think you can handle this alone."

"I have family."

"Yes, but you told me none of them live here. How's that going to work out?"

"It's none of your business!"

"Well, I'm afraid it *is* my business. Like I told you in the beginning, you only have thirty days to get this place cleared so the mold can be removed. Or the city is going to condemn it as unsafe, and you won't be allowed to go in there at all."

Eve waddled toward the porch. "I'll figure it out," she said almost inaudibly.

"For crying out loud, Eve!" Jim ran his hands through his receding hairline with frustration and watched as she somehow made her way up the steps, onto the porch and into the house. Before closing the door hard behind her, she called out, "It's Mrs. Rockford to you."

35: EVE

The nerve of some people! I felt steam coming off my skin from anger. That man! I wanted to slap him to Richmond! Jim Townsend. Who did he think he was, snooping into my private business? I was angry. Frustrated. Humiliated. And was he seriously hitting on me?

I grabbed a yard bag and perched an arm on the kitchen counter, letting my cane fall toward the stool I'd sat on earlier. I picked up a few brown sacks—some pretty colored plastic ones—and stuffed them into the bag. I walked around, holding on to the counter until it ran out and the bag needed to go outside. Unfortunately, it was too full for me to pick up without using both hands. I tried to drag, it but I'd overloaded it. Letting out a nasty sigh, I let go of the counter and heaved the bag up into my arms. I took a step and tripped over something hard on the floor.

My head hit the edge of the stool, and I landed in a pile of tablecloths, placemats, and napkins which cushioned my fall. I reached for my forehead, knowing I'd have a bruise. Rubbing it, I turned my attention to where my cane had landed, half-way across the room. I decided I'd just crawl over there and get it.

"What in blue blazes is going on in here?" Easter's voice was sharp and loud.

I pulled myself up with the cane and stool and looked her in the eye, forgetting about my injury.

"Ow!"

"Eve! Have you been mugged?" Easter quickly made her way to me and reached for my head.

"No! I just lost my balance, that's all."

"Is that the whole story?"

"Why wouldn't it be?"

"Why, indeed," Easter frowned. "I noticed several big bags on the porch. Did you manage to do all that by yourself?"

"No, Jim Townsend did that."

"Well, I'm surprised. I figured those people would be pretty nasty to deal with."

"He was actually nice until he started asking too many personal questions. He even hit on me!"

"Wow! So where's he now?"

"I sent him packing."

"Oh." Easter.

"I'm ready to go home, Easter. I've had enough for today. I've got to find some people with two good legs to help," I said. "No offense intended."

"I hear you, sister."

36

Easter had carved out enough room for Eve to be comfortable and access the walk-in shower in her studio apartment as well. Fresh linens were on the extra bed, and Easter had ordered groceries and already picked them up. She was grateful for that service at a store near her. She still had to get them inside but she had learned to take in the refrigerated and frozen items and come back later to get the rest.

When she had finished showering and dressing, she walked into the small living area to find Eve sobbing with her head in her hands.

"Eve? What's wrong?"

Eve straightened up and wiped her eyes on her long sleeve. "Oh! Sorry, I…I'm just an emotional wreck, Easter."

Easter sat beside her sister on the loveseat. "Are you hurting?"

"Well, I took the pain medicine for the ankle, so it's kicking in. It's not the ankle, Easter. I don't know how to explain it. I just can't get over losing Matt."

Easter got into her face. "Eve, it's been three years!"

"Don't you think I know that? Get outta my face!" She shoved Easter back.

"Look, Eve, I'm not trying to be insensitive, and I've never been married. The only people I've buried were Mama and Daddy. No, I don't understand what you're going through," Easter walked back toward her sister, "but I *do* remember how close you and Matt were and every single time I saw you both, he was grinning from ear to ear. He was so in love with you, Eve. And I can't imagine he'd want you to be so sad. I've never had a love like that," Easter confessed.

Eve turned to her sister, and they hugged and clung to each other for a minute.

"I'm sorry," they said simultaneously.

"But, honey, isn't it wonderful that you loved him that much…so much that your eyes flood with tears and a lump forms in your throat so that you can hardly breathe?"

"I suppose so."

"You were loved that *much*, Eve. I often saw Matt looking at you as though nothing else in the world mattered. You were loved *that* much!"

Eve looked at Easter. "You're right. I was." She managed a smile. "That's not the only thing bothering me, to be honest. Jim Townsend is practically harassing me."

"He's got a job to do, Eve, and you've been avoiding him like the plague. You're going to have to deal with him and your house soon. It's like he said, if he gets pressured by the city, he'll condemn the place, walk away, and you'll be homeless."

"I know," Eve said, bowing her head. "And I guess it's time to bite the bullet."

"I'd say so."

"You seem unusually chipper today," Eve noticed.

"I am. I've been such a Debbie-Downer for too long, and it's not only kept me negative but made me polarizing to other people, especially you, Chris and Hallow. Pat too, but I suppose Chris has taken the brunt of it." She clapped her hands. "Those days are over."

"Huh. What changed?" Eve walked up close to Easter and studied her. "I know! You've met someone, someone who makes you happy." Easter looked sheepish. "Am I right?"

"Yes!" Easter exclaimed, hopping on her best leg. "I have!" She beamed.

"Well, tell me about this guy who's made you happy."

"His name is Keen Proctor. His first name is a family name. Don't you just love it?"

"It's definitely different, and I *do* like it," Eve responded. "How did you meet him?"

"He goes to the same rehab, slash, gym I go to and has the same personal trainer. I'd seen him in there many times, and we smiled at each other but never spoke. He seemed focused on his workout. Anyway, several weeks ago our trainer made a point of introducing us. We have similar problems," Easter said.

"Oh! Is he the guy in the prosthetic leg that works out so hard?"

"Yep. He lost the leg in Afghanistan."

"Oh, so sorry, Easter. But he's a good-looking fella."

"Yes, he is, and he copes well. I guess we were meant to meet because we have so much in common."

"So, he's the reason you're gone so long every other day after you bring me back here?"

"Yeah, we've been practically inseparable ever since we met. We started out going to the gym at the same time, and he just asked if he could take me out. He's a base chaplain, and I'm going with him to church tomorrow and then out to lunch."

"That's awesome!" Eve moved in to hug her sister, pleased with her news. "I'm happy for you, sis."

37

Since Eve was doing fine at Easter's and they still had to finish clearing out the old home place, they decided to meet in Atkinson and finish up that task before putting it up for sale and at least getting that behind them. Chris had never intended cleaning out the old house to take so long. They would discuss Eve's situation then, Chris had decided. All agreed and they picked a non-holiday weekend. Pat would drive his truck, Phyllis would drive separately in her new Lexus, Hallow would drive from Raleigh, and Easter would bring Eve. Chris prayed that they could all get along without anything going awry. It would be nice to have Phyllis pitch in for a change. Chris tried to push down the resentment she felt for her brother and his wife and make this weekend all sweetness even though her fingers and wrists swelled with inflammation and pain again. She seldom mentioned having PsA and how it affected her body. What would be the point? Nobody understood autoimmune diseases like hers. She applied more of the expensive doctor-prescribed cream to them, put on her copper gloves, picked up her overnight bag, and tossed it into the passenger seat.

Once they had all arrived in town, Phyllis hugged each of them. Her blond hair, though shiny and healthy, had started to transition to silver. She wore jeans and a tee-shirt with tiny pink bows on each shoulder and a buffalo check flower in the middle. After exchanging a few words, she stepped forward and made an announcement.

"I am retiring after Christmas! I've already given my notice, so they have plenty of time to find someone to take my place. I'm tired of traveling, and I plan to spend more time with Pat and all of you," she said with a grin. Pat stepped up and hugged her.

"I'm also retiring, and we plan to do some traveling *together* for a change," he said.

"*But*," Phyllis jumped in, holding up a finger, "not until we help you settle all the house stuff."

"Well, I sure do hope we're all finished with this sad business by the end of the year. Congrats to both of you," Chris said.

"Alrighty then!" Easter called out. "Congratulations! Now let's get this show on the road."

"Who's being bossy now?" Hallow called out in jest. They all laughed.

Eve had been quiet, but she went to look through the things piled up with her name at the top as Hallow went through her pile too. "I think I'm going to move east, maybe Wilmington," she announced as she turned toward the others.

"Gosh, it would be great to have you closer, Hallow," Pat said.

"Yeah, there's really not much left in Raleigh to go back to, and I figured I should be able to plan weddings in Wilmington just as well. At least I wouldn't have to move much stuff," she said, her face pruning up.

"Hallow," Eve said, touching her arm, "if you want anything in my house, you can have it. I'm not moving back to Rocky Mount. I may get an apartment near Easter. I'm better off never going back into that place again. And I'm going to go ahead and retire. I've got my years in."

"So you know I was ripped off?"

"Yeah and I told Easter too and threatened her if she made a big deal out of it."

Easter nodded but stayed quiet.

Hallow glanced at Easter and her expression lightened. "That's so sweet of you to offer, Eve, but I don't need much. I've learned all of that stuff isn't so important after all."

Eve waved her hand over her pile. "Well, anyway, you get first dibs. I'm seeing a doctor and she's helping me understand that things aren't as important as people and can never take their place. I mean, I already *knew* that, but somehow I got caught up in sadness, depression and *things*." The sisters hugged.

"You've both been through a lot and I'm glad to see you on the mend," Chris chimed in. "Maybe what Hallow doesn't need or want can be sold."

"Yeah, I know several folks who do yard sales and estate sales sometimes," Phyllis added. "I'd be glad to call them when you're ready, Eve."

Each of them loaded the items with their names attached into their vehicles and then met at the dining room to make final decisions on what was left in the old house. They all agreed that a moth-eaten wool fedora, their mother's makeup, opened bottles of lotion and powders could be trashed along with more ratty purses that had seen better days.

"Geez, Louise! She must have kept every purse she ever had! Let's go through these, though, and make sure she hasn't hidden a million dollars somewhere," Easter said. They grabbed purses and went through outside pockets and zipped inner pockets, finding plenty of Kleenex tissues and a few dollar bills.

"Oh, I think these are the keys to the old Buick," Chris announced, holding up the key ring.

"And here are some old eye-glasses," Eve said, holding them up to her own eyes. "They're about to fall apart."

"Trash," they said in unison.

Pat walked into the kitchen and racked his hands inside a cabinet, coming back with a basket of medications. "Most of these are out-of-date."

"Trash," the girls said.

They each picked out an apron and several scarves their mother had worn over the years.

"If nobody else wants the crochet hooks, knitting needles and embroidery hoops, I think I'd like to have them. There's a group in Jacksonville, and I might join it," Easter told them.

"Yours," three sisters called out.

"How about this easel and Mama's brushes?" Chris asked. When the others shrugged, she added, "I'll take them. I've been toying with the idea of painting, and I have the perfect place to put this. The paints will have to be trashed, though."

Pat walked to the old stereo in the living room. "Does this thing work?"

"I don't think so. You want it?" Chris looked at him quizzically.

"No, I just thought I'd throw it in the back of the truck and haul it off." They all nodded.

"While you're at it, Pat, can you haul off the mattresses? Then we can take down the beds and decide who gets them."

"Sure, Chris. I'll get them another day."

Hallow looked at the two beds before speaking. "I could use both of them or at least one of them."

"Yours," the others called out.

"And, Hallow, why don't you take the bedding that hasn't been spoken for, if nobody cares."

"Fine with me," Easter said.

"Me too," Eve told her sister.

"And you can have the sofa, recliner, and glider rocker as far as I'm concerned," Easter said.

"I don't have a way to move all that stuff," Hallow confessed.

"I'll make sure you get it," Pat told her, touching her wrist. "But it may be a while. Maybe we can leave it right here until you know if you're moving to Wilmington."

"That makes sense, Pat. Thank you. Thank you all, so much. I'm…I'm very appreciative." Hallow dropped her head and the others pretended not to notice.

"If none of you want the garden tiller, I'd like to have it. Maybe I can get the rust off of it and make it useful again around my backyard," Pat said.

Easter wandered over to a little pile of papers. "What's this?

"Oh, those are ration stamps from the Great Depression. I think there're enough for each of us to have some for the sake of history," Chris explained. They all selected a stamp.

"And I have an armful of Bibles. They're well-worn, and Mama wrote in the margins back when she taught Sunday School, I guess. Five in all, one for each of us," Eve announced.

"How wonderful!" Chris called out.

The day had gone well. Pieces of their parents' pasts were in vehicles to go home with them. Other items had been claimed and noted with their name, or labeled to be taken to the Dumpster. Not a single disagreement had ensued.

Everyone hugged as they locked the old house.

38

Hallow and Chris went back to Eve's house a few days later and noticed how much better the porch looked, emptied of all the yard bags. And with Eve's decision not to return to it, the whole process would become easier. Hallow decided to finish up in the kitchen while Chris headed to the master bedroom and bath.

"Ewww!" Hallow raced to the door.

"What's wrong?"

"Roaches! Roaches all over the kitchen, in the cabinets, on the floor, and they're big enough to carry me off. This place is totally infested!"

Chris walked toward her. "I'm not surprised with all these boxes, especially pizza boxes. I don't understand why she kept the boxes."

"Me either," Hallow commented.

"I just cut my way through a bunch of huge spider webs in the den and bedroom. I'm surprised she isn't covered with whelps or worse. A brown recluse spider would eat her flesh," Chris said, realizing how loud her voice had become. "The carpet is beyond saving. Totally disgusting! I just think the whole house needs to be torn down with all this crap in it."

"Or burned," Hallow added as she touched the side of her head. "Hey, why don't we just hire somebody to empty the place and we won't have to deal with it? Do you think Eve would go for that?"

"It's possible, I suppose," Chris replied, "but don't get your hopes up."

They both turned as a red truck drove up behind their vehicles. A man got out and approached them.

"Hello," he said.

"Hello," they responded in unison. "Can we help you with something?"

"Um, I was hoping Eve was here." They stared. "Oh, I'm Jim Townsend, an inspector for the city. Eve…Mrs. Rockford and I have met, and I was hoping we could continue our conversation about this situation." He pointed toward the house.

"So you're aware," Chris said.

"Yes. I came over and helped her one day, but I apparently upset her, and she made it pretty clear that she wanted no more help from me. Now she's not responding to any of my calls."

Chris and Hallow looked at one another. "We'll try to light a fire under her, Mr. Townsend," Chris told him.

39

September

With a low-pressure system on the Florida coast threatening to become a tropical storm, the siblings all brought boxes and newspapers to pack up everything small left in the old house and take it home with them. Then they would decide what happened to the big heavy furniture and have the house professionally cleaned and put on the market to sell. They all wore shorts because even though a light wind blew, the air held enough humidity to soak through clothing and make them all sticky and miserable. Alerts on their phones signaled a tornado warning had been issued for southwestern Pender County.

"I packed an overnight bag and plan to stay since it might be rough in Wilmington by Sunday," Pat told them.

"I did too," Chris said. "It's certain to get rough in Morehead."

Easter, Eve and Hallow had also stuck bags in just in case they were better off staying rather than driving in heavy rain and wind later in the afternoon. They had learned years earlier not to fully depend on the forecast. Sometimes the meteorologists were wrong. Even with all the high-tech equipment, Mother Nature fooled them quite often.

Each of the Hollidays found things that were marked as theirs and wrapped fragile glass and dishes in paper before tucking them into boxes for safe travel.

Pat looked up at the attic door as he passed. "Um, did we ever check the attic for stuff?"

Chris put her hands on her hips. "You know, we've talked about it quite a few times but I don't think we ever did."

Pat pulled the cord, lowering the folded stairs to the floor, not prepared for the avalanche of plastic food containers that pelted him. As he backed away, they watched in amazement as the floor filled up.

"For the love of Pete!"

After ducking the avalanche, they broke into laughter and began picking them up. "Let's count 'em," Hallow said. They all agreed and stacked them in piles for counting. Then Pat climbed into the attic to see if there were more.

"Wait! I'm throwing more down. It's unbelievable up here!"

Eve and Hallow held a large black trash bag and caught the bag full, handed it off, and got another one and then another one.

"My question is 'why?'" Easter asked.

"Mother came up during the Depression and I guess she just couldn't throw things away," Hallow explained.

"That's true, but she was *also* impulsive at times and threw some things away that she needed later. Don't you remember, Chris?"

"Oh yeah. So, I guess the Depression wasn't exactly the reason." Pat climbed down with a dusty brown suitcase in his hand.

"This is the only thing left up there besides books covered in dust and cobwebs," he said. The suitcase was empty.

"Well, let's get this mess counted and out of here," Easter said. They began their count and added the ones they'd counted into black bags too.

"The grand total is, drum roll please," Easter said with the pad in her hand, "Seven hundred and thirty-six!"

"And they're going straight to the trash," Chris added, looking directly at Eve, who nodded. She looked around for Pat and saw him climbing back into the attic.

"Pat, what are you doing?"

"I want to see what these books are," she heard him call out. "Sometimes people have first editions they don't even know they have. They could be worth a lot of money."

"Well, we need to get all these bags out of here," she added.

"When the wind calms down, I'll put them in my truck and haul them off," he offered.

Easter picked up her phone. "It certainly hasn't rained much and the wind isn't nearly as bad as I thought it would be," she said, checking the weather.

"Where's the storm now?" Chris asked her.

"My phone weather shows a bad cell coming right at us, predicted to be in our location at 3 pm." They all looked at the time. It was 2:49.

"Hey, Pat, you might want to get out of the attic," Eve called up.

"In a minute."

"*Now!*"

He peeked over the edge at them.

"Storm. Here. Now. Get down here!"

He quickly backed down the narrow attic stairs and followed his sisters, who scurried to the tiny bathroom and huddled. Easter sat on the edge of the tub, and Eve and Hallow sat down on the tile floor. Chris and Pat crouched just inside the door after it was closed. Even though there was a window, it was the safest place in the house since there was no basement. All eyes were on the window while the only sound was the wind roaring overhead.

"Look! That's a funnel going across the sky!" Easter pointed.

"It sure is, but at least it didn't drop on us," Pat said, hoping to calm fears.

They stayed in the bathroom until the wind died down a few minutes later.

"Maybe it's safe to get out?" Chris didn't sound too sure.

"Who's got a phone?" Pat pulled his out. "The radar looks clear for us but bad for Burgaw. I think we're safe at least for a few minutes. Some outer bands of the storm are getting close, though."

Once they were back in the living room, they took a minute to calm themselves and look through the windows to the outside. Even though the yard was full of small limbs and leaves, there didn't seem to be any damage.

"I'll check our vehicles to make sure they're okay." Pat headed for the door.

"That was a little scary," Hallow commented. Her three sisters nodded.

Once Pat came in and reported no damage to any cars or trucks, he wanted to go back in the attic.

"I'll check for leaks while I'm up there."

"What *is* up there, Pat?"

Pat told them that he had found novels which might have been be in great shape if they had been boxed up or protected in some way, but they hadn't been. He climbed back up the flimsy attic stairs and grabbed a handful of books. He wiped dust from them to read their titles: *David Copperfield, The Magic Mountain, The Complete Works of William Shakespeare, To Kill A Mockingbird, The Great Gatsby, Little Women, 1984, Pride and Prejudice, Jane Eyre, Wuthering Heights,* and *The Grapes of Wrath.* Other books were in such poor shape he couldn't read the titles and their pages were yellowed and coming apart. Still others had been wet at some point.

"Toss me up a bag to put these in, please," he shouted to his sisters below.

"Find any first editions?" Eve asked, tossing up a bag.

"Nah. Lots of classics but nothing valuable."

"Mama joined some kind of book club that mailed her a book a month," Chris remembered. "I guess these are some of them." When Pat dropped the bag into Eve's hands the sisters peeked in and checked them out.

"Oh, I'd love to read *Little Women* again," Easter said. "I adored that book."

"Me too," Eve said. "Can I read it after you?"

"Sure, we'll pass some of these around. Let's not throw any of the good ones out," Hallow added.

As Pat reached the floor, he said, "Well, the others aren't worth taking down. They are coming apart, and I'm just going to leave them up there. But I do want to read *1984* again and see how it compares to the present." They all nodded.

Suddenly the outer storm bands crashed on them, and the house creaked and snapped, thunder boomed, and lightning lit up the dark sky. They covered hurting ears from the sudden drop in barometric pressure. Rain rolled off the roof in heavy sheets. Unless the storm moved through quickly, flooding would be their next problem.

Pat pulled up the radar on his phone. Though the storm was not wide, it was ferocious, and the rain could train over them for hours. The deep ditch across the street was full of debris moving quickly over the banks, powered by fast-moving water and high wind. They could only hunker down and pray that the old roof stayed on and didn't leak like a sieve. They quieted and found a place to try to get as comfortable as possible to wait it out.

"Good news!" Hallow reported, jarring the rest from semi-sleep. "The storm is predicted to turn out to sea, so we shouldn't have to worry about a major hurricane."

"That *is* good news," Pat said with a smile. "The rain has eased up, too."

"It's already turning east, but the rip currents are terrible between Wilmington and the Outer Banks according to my phone's weather."

"It must have come up this far and turned right on top of us," Chris said.

"Well, at least we didn't get torn apart," Pat added with relief in his voice.

Chris and Easter both nodded with relief.

40: EASTER

The next morning Eve went to the doctor in Jacksonville, and he told her she could start driving a little bit around Jacksonville. That was all the news she needed to head all the way to Atkinson to pick up the rest of the items she'd chosen. Since she was driving again, I decided to stay put. I needed some time without her. I'd been used to being alone, and when she moved in with me, I got out of whack. Nothing stayed organized and where I'd always kept it. I'd told her repeatedly to stay out of my bedroom and to keep her personal things in *her* room. Still, I continued to find her things strewn all over the small kitchen and living area. I was ready for her to go home or find a place of her own. But I hesitated to be honest with her because of her 'condition' as Chris called it.

I had talked to Keen about my feelings since he had a psychology degree so I decided to head to the gym and work off some stress and tension. Hopefully I'd be in a better mood when Eve returned. She was the only person I'd told about Keen. I could easily ruin a relationship in one evening, but so far, things were pleasant, and I had not shown him my nasty side. I guess I hoped that working out with a good-looking gym friend who happened to be a chaplain might improve my disposition.

41

Eve had enjoyed the drive to Atkinson and handled the old Acadia as if she'd never been away from the steering wheel. It was also nice to get away from Easter and the small apartment space she was allotted. It was time to either go home—which she didn't want to do—or find a new place to live, maybe around Jacksonville or Morehead City. She wasn't sure she wanted to deal with Wilmington and the nightmarish traffic, and Raleigh was totally out of the question for the same reason. A sudden knock on the old house's front door startled her and she hobbled over with her cane to open it. The Atkinson Baptist pastor stood there in a green and navy plaid shirt, grinning.

"Ah, Mr. Stone," Eve said, trying to push a lock of hair from her face. "Your unexpected visit has caught me at my absolute worst." His face flushed as she made eye contact with the handsome man.

"Not at all. A beautiful woman like yourself needs no enhancements," he said with a smile. "I *do* apologize for not calling, but, well, I don't have your phone number, and the house phone has apparently been disconnected."

"Yes, it has." Eve hobbled toward a chair on the front porch. "Please have a seat. What brings you over?"

He walked to her mother's old swing and tested the chains before sitting and swinging gently, a hand on each hand rail.

"I could fib and say I was just passing by but—"

"But you're a preacher, and you don't lie," Eve interrupted. She began to feel vulnerable and wondered if her siblings had anything to do with his visit while she was at the old house alone. Was he going to try to pray her out of hoarding? Did he even know about it? Or was he only paying a visit to someone who'd been injured?

"I try to be honest at all times." He looked down, seeming to be uncomfortable, now wringing his hands.

"Did my sisters put you up to coming over here?" Eve scowled. "I can tell you right now that

I'm fine. I will get over this injury, and then I will get my house and my life back together. I don't need your help."

"Your sisters? Why no. I haven't spoken to any of them I... just heard you were here today, and I wanted to stop by. Should they have talked to me?" He looked puzzled.

"No, they certainly shouldn't. I mean. I'm fine." Eve stood. "Look, Mr. Stone, I need to finish what I came to do and head back to Jacksonville before dark."

"Oh!" He stood too. "Well, I'd heard that you were in an accident and had a stint in rehab. I'm glad to see that you're mending well." He nodded at her ankle. "I don't mean to keep you from your tasks but, well, I was wondering . . ."

"Wondering *what*?" Eve snapped at him. He cleared his throat.

"Well, um, I know this is out of the blue, but I did hear that you were single, and I—"

"I'm a *widow*," Eve added with a harsh tone.

He lifted his shaky fingers to his brows and kneaded them, his nerves seeming to fray.

"Look, I'm sorry. I'm doing a terrible job of trying to get your phone number. It's been a long time since I wanted a lady's number."

"*What*?"

"Your phone number. I'd like to call you sometime…I mean, if it's okay, that is." Eve stared at him. "Maybe take you out to dinner?" His face now wore worry.

Eve felt her face flush with heat. "I don't know. I mean, I don't date, Mr. Stone."

"Please call me Mark. We don't have to call it a date. I didn't mean to upset you. I'm not good at this, as you can tell. It's just that as a single guy myself and a preacher at that, I seldom get to spend time with ladies other than church members, most of whom are married or way too old for me."

He walked to the steps. "I've bungled this badly. I should go." He turned toward the porch steps and then hesitated and turned around with a nervous jerk. "I just thought that the Sunday you came to church with your family maybe you and I had kind of um…connected on some level. I don't know. Perhaps I imagined it. But can I give you *my* number in case you'd consider having dinner with me? No strings attached, of course. Just a friendly meal. I'd be happy to drive to Jacksonville. It's not far down highway 53, as you, no doubt, already know." He cleared his throat and pulled at his collar. "There's not much to eat around here unless I cook, and you probably don't want to go there." He laughed, and Eve reluctantly joined in, accepting the card with his name and number. She figured she could toss it out later.

Eve remained silent, and he nodded and walked down the steps and over to his black truck. She hobbled back into the house and gathered up a few more things that were hers now. She supposed she was the liar. After all, she wasn't supposed to be driving this far out of Jacksonville. She just simply needed some time away from Easter, the mistress of her domain. She supposed she felt the same way once about her own space. Now her house and life were so out of control that she shivered at the thought. She guessed Easter was afraid that she'd ruin her apartment too. That wasn't going to happen, though. She threw her head up. I was stronger now. I was going to conquer this sick turn of events and come out on the other side. She pushed the pastor's card into the side pocket of her purse and picked up her beach bag, ready to get back to Jacksonville and elevate her swelling ankle.

42: PAT

I decided to call my sisters and let them know I'd like to go to the old rustic cabin in the woods that Daddy had built when I was a teenager. None of them had a problem with it, and none of them wanted to accompany me since there was only a generator for power and a one-hole outhouse. I felt relieved to be able to have some time there alone without any sister drama. I packed a small bag just in case I decided to spend the night although I'd never been much of a woodsman.

I unlocked the fence gate and drove on to the primitive cabin, scattering wild turkeys as I drove into the clearing and parked. I heard a ruckus and turned in time to see two white tails running away from me. I smiled. This was Daddy's favorite get-away back in the day. He loved to come here with friends for a night or two, and I came along occasionally just to spend time with him without the girls and Mama. We usually gathered wood and had a campfire even in warm weather. Daddy roasted hot dogs and made s'mores. I cherished that memory.

Considering its age, the cabin was still in fairly good shape. Unlocking the wide wood door, I scraped away thick spider webs, and leaned on the doorjamb to look around inside the two-story shelter with a rusted pot-bellied stove and let more memories consume me. It still amazed me that my father—a small-framed man—had been able to build this all by himself. He had little money tied up in it because his brother had given him two old tobacco barns that were about to be bull-dozed. He'd torn them down and moved them piece by piece to rebuild in the space he'd cleared and graded. Daddy had numbered each piece so he could reconstruct the barn once he moved it with nothing but a trailer and his bare hands. Friends had donated cast-off doors, windows that didn't match, and two hide-a-bed sofas. He'd even managed to wrangle roof tin from an old hunting buddy.

Somehow, he turned all the odds and ends into a comfortable cabin with a sleeping loft. His brother-in-law, my uncle, had offered an unused pot-belly stove which became the central cooking stove and winter warmth. Above the stove and around most of the walls an array of eyes stared at me. Stuffed bobcats, mounted deer heads, and one large bass added to the cabin's ambience even though they were covered in dust and spider webs. Cabinets had been installed here and there to store pots and pans. Daddy had learned early on not to leave corn meal and flour in them, so most of the space now stored sleeping bags and items that didn't attract bugs. I pulled at a small folding table leaning on the wall and wiped it off before setting it up. I placed my snacks and bag on it. As old as this place was, and as long as it had been empty, I still felt Daddy's presence here. I smiled.

43

Early November

Eve instructed Jim Townsend as he held up items for her to view.

"Trash," she said.

She had reluctantly allowed Jim—who had managed to get her an extension—to help her tackle the piles of stuff. She didn't really have a choice. It was either Jim or someone else from the city who would condemn and lock up the house, her house. If she wanted to make decisions, she could wait no longer. The city had lost patience with her insincere promises to clean it up.

Eve's cell phone trilled. She didn't recognize the number but decided to answer anyway. "Hello?"

"Mom!"

"Kirsten?"

"Mom, I'm coming home! Back to North Carolina!" Her ecstatic daughter announced.

"Oh! *Really?* That's wonderful news! When?"

"I'll be home for Thanksgiving." Eve suddenly saw the room spin and latched on to Jim Townsend, who stood nearby. "Mom? Mom, isn't that great? I can celebrate with the family this year," Kirsten said.

"Yes, um, of course, honey. That's awesome news. Give me the details," Eve said with as much enthusiasm as she could muster. She held on to Jim and glanced around at her house. Kirsten's house. They talked for a few minutes, and when they were finished, Eve's face had a look of panic.

"What's wrong?" Jim stared at her and held her arms as she wobbled.

"My daughter is coming home from Germany."

"Well, isn't that *great?*"

"No! Jim, look at this house. I can't let her see this. What am I going to do?"

"Calm down," Jim told her, settling her on the edge of a chair. "How soon is she coming?"

"Thanksgiving! That's only three weeks away, Jim!" Eve snatched at her hair, and he took both her hands in his.

"Eve, listen to me. We can do this. We can pull off cleaning out this mess if you're willing," he said with a soft voice. "But you've gotta trust me."

Eve nodded. "I *do*, but in three weeks? It's impossible, Jim." Their eyes surveyed the rooms they could see, knowing the others were just as bad or worse.

"I have a truck and access to lots of friends with trucks. If you'll allow me, I will get'em organized in such a way that you can bundle up, sit in a chair outside, and decide what happens to everything." He paced in front of her, looking at his phone. "You might want to see if your sisters can help too. We'll need all hands on deck."

"Yes! I'll call them right now."

He knelt in front of her with concern written on his face. "But Eve, are you *sure* about this? Are you sure you're up to getting rid of so much at one time?"

"Yes, I am," Eve declared. "I have to admit there's not much here worth saving, and she's more important to me than anything in this house. It's all done with. I'm just done."

He smiled. "Okay. How soon do you want to start?"

"Tomorrow," Eve said standing again. "You line up your guys and I'll call Chris and Hallow." She reached out to him and hesitantly hugged him and he hugged back. "Thank you so much, Jim." Their eyes held for a moment.

"10-4, good buddy," he said with a salute and a broad smile before filling another bag with trash.

44: EVE

I was flabbergasted and my head spun with panic, but Jim walked outside to call his truck buddies and I dialed Chris and listened impatiently as her phone rang and finally went to voicemail.

"Chris, it's Eve. Please call me as soon as you get this message. It's urgent!" She pressed OFF sure that her message would no doubt scare Chris when she got it. Moving on, she dialed Hallow.

"Eve! How are you?"

"Oh, Hallow! You've got to come. Please help me!"

"What on earth's wrong? Did something fall on you again?"

"No. It's Kirsten."

"Oh no! Oh no!" I could hear my sister moving around.

"No, no, she's not injured. She's coming *home*," I explained.

"Wh…what?" There was a pause. "Well, aren't you glad? Isn't that good?"

"No, Hallow! You know what this house looks like. I can't let her see it like this."

"Oh. Yeah, right. So how soon—?"

"Thanksgiving. She'll be home for Thanksgiving," I said with the panic now gone and shock taking its place.

"Okay. Let me sit down and mull this over," Hallow said.

"Jim Townsend, the inspector? He was here when Kirsten called, trying to help me form a plan. He's outside now calling some men to come and help get everything—and I do mean *everything*—out of this house."

"Well, that's good."

"But I need you, Chris, and Pat to help too." I could hear pleading in my voice.

"What's the plan?"

"Well, Jim said he'd bundle me up in a chair outside and as they haul stuff out, I can tell them what to do with it. That's the fastest way, Hallow. We need those areas you mentioned. You know, one for trash, one for what I want to keep, another one for stuff that will go somewhere else."

"Are you sure, Eve?"

"I'm sure. I'm okay, Hallow. Please come as soon as you can. If we can get all this mess out of

here, I can have a painter come in and at least
make the house look and smell better. Fingers
crossed."

"Well, I guess I'll try to come tomorrow. Chris
and I can get a room at the hotel again. If Pat
can get off work, he has a big truck too."

"Yeah, I left Chris a message, and I'm calling
Pat next. Easter just can't handle this, so she can
sit outside with me.

"Okay. I'll pack a bag and take care of a few
things here. See you tomorrow," Hallow said as
she clicked off. My phone sounded, and it was
Chris.

"Chris!"

"Eve, what's going on?" Chris's voice sounded
stressed.

"Calm down. I'm sorry I sounded so panicked
in my message. I'm calmer now," I said.

"About what?"

"Kirsten called this morning, very excited. She's
coming home."

"How wonderful!"

"No, Chris. This house. This mess. She'll be
home for Thanksgiving," I added.

"Oh, my. What do you need for me to do?" I
could always count on Chris.

"Can you come? Hallow's coming and I'm
going to call Pat too. Maybe he can take off a few
days. I don't know. Anyway, Jim Townsend, the
inspector, was here when Kirsten called, and he's

outside now trying to line up some men with trucks to come and clean out the house."

"Are you sure you're alright with that?"

"Yes! I'm fine! Why does everyone keep asking me that? I guess it took a shock to start hoarding and it's taken another one to stop. I don't know. All I can say is I'm over this dump, and I don't want Kirsten to see any of this. I feel like I drove her away after Matt died and when I started, um, bringing stuff in, she moved out. I can't let this come between us anymore."

"I understand, and I'm proud of you. I need to do some things here today, but I should be able to come tomorrow. I'll call Hallow and we can coordinate on lodging for a few days."

"Thanks so much, Chris. I knew I could count on you," I said sincerely.

I talked to Pat, and he said he'd take off Tuesday, Wednesday, and Thursday since Phyllis was on her last official trip before retiring. Jim lined up four other men to help at different times during the week. One of them also painted houses as a second job. I was relieved that Chris had volunteered to host Thanksgiving at her home in Morehead. At least Kirsten could fly in and go there before coming to Rocky Mount, buying me more time. Maybe.

45

The Holliday siblings had tried helping, avoiding, postponing, and finally negotiating with Eve over her hoarding. Jim had made a small amount of headway with her through suggestions, intimidation, or outright threats. Still Kirsten unknowingly caused the panic that got things moving out of her house. Pat, Hallow, Chris, and Easter all showed up early with thermoses of coffee and one for Eve, who was already bundled in the yard chaise. Jim laid huge blue tarps on the lawn and tagged them with signs. Three other men had arrived with pickup trucks, and all backed in to make the removal process easier.

Easter sat beside Eve to stay out of the way and support her sister. Everyone had been instructed to let Eve see what came out of the house piece by piece and make her own decision. In the beginning it was easy enough for her to call out "trash" because most of it was boxes, papers, drink cans or bottles that nobody wanted.

"Let's put all the cans and bottles in a pile for recycling," one man suggested. She nodded. The entire morning yielded trucks filled with loads to take to the landfill and the animal shelter. The "save" tarp had little on it, but once they'd removed the real trash, the decisions became more complicated. They stopped to eat pizzas Easter had ordered and gone to pick up. The men were hungry with big appetites, and she was glad she'd ordered seven large ones with various toppings.

Most of the kitchen appliances would go to the landfill, and Eve settled on two stock pots and one skillet that was hidden in a cabinet and in good shape. The rest she waved away.

"The Salvation Army will most likely take the pots and pans," Jim called out to her as he carried a pile to the edge of another tarp. Once they'd emptied the kitchen, the next task was to tackle the den. The bookcase that had fallen on Eve had cracked and she pointed to the trash pile for that.

"What about all the books, Eve?" Chris asked.

"I want to go through them. Put them here in front of Easter and me, and we'll decide." Hallow and Chris carried armloads to the other two sisters while men wrestled with a sofa that was badly stained, worn, and stank.

"Haul that thing off too," Eve said. She kept end tables and let an upholstered chair go since it had been stained beyond usefulness. The mattress she'd been sleeping on had a well-worn cavity in the middle where she'd slept, surrounded by piles that could have killed her. She turned red when it appeared. Jim and a helper took it straight to the landfill pile.

"I guess I'm going to have to buy almost everything new, Easter."

"It's okay. Maybe you can find a furnished apartment or at least take your time selecting new things that you truly love," Easter whispered as she picked up another stack of books to go through.

"This is too much. I think I'll just keep the hard covers and let the paperbacks go," Eve said, looking over tall piles of books.

"Good idea. Many of them are yellowed and have torn pages, and some don't even have a cover. I'll toss these over there in the trash pile unless I think they're good enough to sell," Easter told her. "Maybe we can have a yard sale in Jacksonville and get a little bit out of them."

"No, Easter. I just want to get rid of the past. I need a new beginning for the most part."

"We've got unopened boxes of air fryers and two microwaves. What do you want us to do with them?" Her sisters studied her.

"I don't know."

"Why on earth?"

Eve waved Hallow's question away. "I bought them for wedding gifts or Christmas presents. Maybe Kirsten can use some of them," she quickly added.

Her bedroom suite was in reasonably good shape although scratches were evident when it passed by. Most of the bedding went to the trash area unless it had been stored in the chest of drawers and looked acceptable. The bureau dresser came out next and men set it down in front of Eve. She stood and limped to the furniture, pulling out drawers that revealed a plethora of jewelry. She and Easter glanced at each other.

"How many pearl necklaces is this?" Easter started picking up strands and putting them over her arm. "Twelve strings of pearls, almost identical? Where on earth did you get these?"

"Home Shopping Network," Eve eked out with a red face.

"Oh my gosh!" Easter said loud enough to turn heads. She then quieted to spare Eve further embarrassment.

Pat walked over with the dresser's matching mirror. "This'll have to be reattached when you decide where it goes. It's in great shape except for the dust," he added. "We'll soon have enough out that you can walk through, Eve, since you don't need your cane much anymore."

Eve smiled and nodded. A man brought a pile of baskets over for her to go through. Easter looked at the collection and snatched up one from her mother's house.

"Wait!" Easter stared. "Wait just a minute. How did *this* get here?" She glared at Eve. "This was supposed to *mine!* You took it, Eve. When? Why did you take it? You knew it was mine! We all agreed that I could have this one."

Eve backed up and sat down in her chaise, as everyone outside stopped and looked at them. She rested her forehead on knuckles, ashamed and overwhelmed, choking back tears. "I can't do this anymore." She stood and headed toward her car.

"Eve, where are you going?" Jim called out. She looked around at him with his sweat-filled curls.

"I'm done! Discard it, put it in a pile to donate, or store it. At the rate we're going, it'll take months to clean out, and I don't have months! Do whatever you want with it, Jim. I am just done," she called out sadly with her head lowered. She glanced at Easter, who had her hands on her hips and she knew the conversation between them wasn't over. She started her old Acadia and drove away from all of them.

46: EASTER

Even though workers continued to haul out furniture, curtains, and everything that they could, I decided to head to Jacksonville too, and confront my sister. How dare she steal from me, and I'm housing her! I told Chris, Pat, and Hallow I was leaving too. They wanted me to take Eve's clothes that were mold-free. The rest would go onto a tarp labeled "mold." I hesitantly took an armful and threw them in the back seat of my bug. Eve could dig them out herself. I picked up Mama's basket that I'd marked back at the old house and put it beside me in the passenger seat. I would be keeping my eyes on it from now on.

I stopped at Parker's Barbecue in Wilson and got a sandwich and fries to eat on the way back. I didn't get Eve anything. She could find her own food. I was determined not to have a melt down on the way home and go into my own house ranting and raving, so I did my best to calm down because I knew she'd be all to pieces. I didn't know whether to be mad with her or pity her. Self-control had never been in my wheel house and apparently wasn't in Eve's either.

I knew Keen Proctor well enough now to discuss my anger issues and he had helped me with some tips like taking deep breaths to stay calm, and how to be in tune with my emotions enough to recognize when I was about to blow a gasket. Free therapy. I started breathing exercises now in hopes of being calm when I pulled into my driveway.

The gray-sided apartment came into view, and I took another long breath. I asked God to keep me calm regardless of Eve's emotional state. I decided to leave the basket in the VW until later and walked to the door, expecting it to be locked. It wasn't. I opened it and peeked inside. Eve wasn't in sight, so I took another slow breath and went in as though nothing had happened. Eve's bedroom door was closed but I could hear her sobbing. I decided to leave her alone until she was strong enough to have the conversation that had to take place. I slipped on my gym shoes and locked the door behind me, hoping a little workout would relieve my tension. And Keen might be there, which would make exercising more pleasant.

47: EVE

I'd cried all the way from Rocky Mount to Jacksonville, sobbing to the point that I could barely see the highway's center line. I played back all the embarrassment from the nasty mattress to mouse droppings and filthy roaches running across items as they carried them outside. I couldn't look any of them in the eye again. All of them were things from my home, and it horrified me. What must Chris, Hallow, and Pat think of me? And Jim? And all the men he'd found to help?

I'd forgotten about Mama's basket. I couldn't blame Easter for being upset with me. We had both placed a colored Post-it note on quite a few of the baskets and flipped a coin on that one. I lost. But at some point, I must have put it with my things. I don't know. I don't remember doing it intentionally, but it *was* at my house. I never answered Easter's question about the pearls either. Not *really*. I sometimes got carried away on those shopping networks that make it so easy to buy. I'd initially thought I'd give some away as gifts because they were such a reasonable price, but I never did. I had a short pearl necklace that I wore quite often, but the rest were just laying there in a drawer. Although she didn't open any more drawers, she would have found many more similar things I'd bought over the past three years.

I pushed myself up off the wet pillow and wiped my eyes and blew my nose. I thought I heard Easter's Beetle, and I'd better prepare myself for her wrath. I ran into the bathroom and wiped my face with a cold cloth as I heard the exterior door close. I took a deep breath and opened the door and walked into the small living area. Nobody was there. Then I heard her VW driving away. She'd been home and left again.

I looked in the fridge and found some deli meat and made myself a simple sandwich, grabbing some chips to have with it. I guzzled a can of Pepsi and thought about Kirsten, coming home to find out how far I had descended down a dark path since she left. I hoped Jim and my siblings would just get rid of the whole mess. Even though I should be helping them, I didn't feel strong enough to do it.

Kirsten. Home in a couple of weeks. Part of me could hardly wait to see her. After Matt died and I began hoarding, she moved out, and then I had to see her off to the military on a stormy day. It nearly killed me. She was so young! I supposed I'd neglected her and her needs as a young lady. Another piece of sadness wrapped around me. I had to find a way to make things right with her. It was embarrassing enough for her to have a mother as old as I was without all the other issues attached. I had to get a grip and see the house emptied, mold removed, and the whole interior painted, and time was not on my side. I had to make things right with Easter first, though. Where on earth had she gone?

I called Chris to see how things were going and asked her to apologize to everyone else. She said the men had hauled away all the trash and landfill items, and she'd called The Salvation Army to pick up another tarp loaded with donated items. Jim would store the furniture at a town facility until I could decide on each piece, and Hallow was going through the clothes to see what could be salvaged and what needed to be trashed. Her voice seemed strained but I couldn't blame her. And she…they *all* had to be exhausted by now. I thanked her and clicked *Off.*

❀ ❀ ❀

I stood when I heard Easter drive up. I had taken a shower and refreshed my mind, body and spirit as best I could. I waited for her to get into the room.

"Oh, you're up," Easter said in an unexpectedly pleasant voice.

"Yes." We made eye contact for what seemed like forever but had to be only seconds. I could feel tears flooding my eyes. "Easter, I'm so sorry. I don't know what else to say."

She nodded and a smile appeared and disappeared quickly. "Have you had anything to eat, Eve?"

"Yeah, I fixed a sandwich and chips. You?"

"I stopped at Parker's and got a sandwich. I guess we can make do tonight then."

"Yes, I just ate a few minutes ago." Eve looked at her cell phone and realized it was nearly five o'clock.

Easter plowed into her recliner and kicked off her shoes.

"Did you go to the gym?"

"I did. I needed to get rid of some tension and frustration," Easter said bringing her eyes up to meet mine.

"Easter, I just don't know where to begin. I need to make things right," I started.

"Don't worry about it. I got my basket back."

"It's not just about the basket. It's *everything*! I'm not sure how I ended up with that basket, but I *must* have taken it. Otherwise it wouldn't be in my stuff. I'm appalled that I'd do something like that to you. To *anybody*." I kept my voice low and controlled.

"It's okay, Eve," Easter said calmly.

"How come you're so calm about this now?"

"I've had time to calm down. The gym helped."

"Good. Maybe I should start going. Was your friend there?"

"Keen? Yes, he came in about the time I was going to leave, so I talked to him a while."

"He seems to have a positive effect on you. I'd like to meet him."

"Maybe you should," Easter said, trying to get out of the recliner. "We *do* need to talk about our living arrangement, Eve. You're doing well now and I just saw that there's an apartment on the next block for rent. It won't be available long with all the military families around. You should look in to it."

"I will. I know I've disrupted your life by moving in here and I do thank you. But you're right. It's time for me to say goodbye to Rocky Mount and that whole situation and start my life over. I just don't think I can pull it off before Kirsten gets home."

"I stopped by that apartment and peeked in the window on my way home It's furnished, at least enough that you could move in right away. You just need a mattress," Easter said.

"Really? Wow! That sounds great. Maybe I could do that. And Kirsten could come to Jacksonville instead of going to Rocky Mount." Some confidence crept back.

"My thoughts exactly. A win-win situation," my sister said with a grin.

48

Thanksgiving

Chris's house was decorated with beautiful fall colors and scintillating aromas wafted through all three levels. Hallow, Easter, Pat, Phyllis, and Eve all arrived early to greet Kirsten with yellow ribbons in the scruffy brush trees near the house. She'd fly in to the Wilmington airport and rent a car, although Pat had offered to pick her up and bring her. Eve had invited Jim since he'd come through with getting the Rocky Mount house emptied, had the mold issue taken care of, and even had a painter in the process of painting the interior. Items she wanted to keep he'd brought to a Jacksonville storage facility. She was grateful for his help and owed him, she figured. She was glad he'd had a haircut and his curls were much more manageable.

The relief was evident on Eve's face, along with plenty of excitement. Her retirement was official and she had moved into the two-bedroom apartment near Easter. She would go through her furniture and add pieces later. Those decisions were pushed to the background now that Kirsten was practically on Chris's doorstep.

They were gathered in the kitchen when they heard someone running up the stairs and quickly turned to see Kirsten bounce into the room with arms stretched out to hug each of them. A young man walked up behind her and stood, smiling as she greeted her mother, aunts, and her uncle.

"I'm so excited to be here!" Kirsten's voice bubbled with delight as she pulled her long brunette hair back from her eyes. She turned to motion the young man forward. "Everyone, this is Will Lowe. My fiancé!"

Eve teetered and grabbed Jim's arm. "Wh...what?"

"Wow! Hi, Will. Welcome to my home," Chris said stepping forward to hug him after glancing at Eve.

"Congratulations," Hallow and Easter said simultaneously.

Will nodded, still smiling, as Pat shook his hand. "Welcome to the family, Will."

"Thank you, sir. Thank you all," he said with a shaky voice. He also looked toward Eve but said nothing. He had black hair and a clean-shaven face that lit up as he turned his eyes back to Kirsten. He wore a black crew neck sweater.

"Aunt Hallow, we want you to help us plan the wedding," Kirsten said to her aunt.

"I'd love that! Have you set a date?"

"Yes, we want a Christmas wedding!"

"Next Christmas?"

"No," Kirsten answered, looking around at everyone in the room and resting her eyes on Eve. "*This* Christmas. Christmas Eve, actually." She smiled at Will.

Hallow stepped toward her with Eve alongside. "Wait! You mean like the Christmas Eve that's a month away? *That* Christmas?"

Kirsten laughed. "Yes. I know you can do it, Aunt Hallow."

"But Kirsten," Eve said taking her daughter's hand. "This is so sudden. It takes months to plan a wedding, honey. Even Hallow with her experience can't possibly—"

"I know you can pull this off, Aunt Hallow," Kirsten interrupted, giving her aunt a pleading look. "And mom, we've known each other for two years. It's not sudden for us. We just didn't want to get married without our families with us to celebrate. It'll be small and intimate. No big frills. I hope we can get Atkinson Baptist Church where you all grew up even though I only visited there a few times. It has such beautiful stained-glass windows and there's a fellowship hall for the reception." In the next breath, "Will's grandmother will be coming from Japan." The Holliday family glanced at Will, picking up a hint of Asian blood.

"Well, I, um." Hallow unlocked her eyes from her niece's and glanced at Eve who was trembling. "Why don't we eat our Thanksgiving feast and then we can discuss this some more?"

Chris, Pat, Phyllis, Easter, and Jim had retreated to near the kitchen counter, listening to the exchange. "Then dinner is served," Chris announced. "Phyllis, will you put ice in the glasses?"

"Sure."

Chris had set up a buffet along the long counter, and food filled all open spaces. Ham, turkey and dressing, gravy, rice, collards, turnips, corn, sweet potato casserole, yeast rolls, and a wide assortment of desserts would, no doubt, leave no one hungry. The family ate, chatting all along with Will and Jim, who couldn't keep his eyes off Eve.

"So, where are you from, Will?"

Swallowing his food, he responded, "Goldsboro. Seymour-Johnson Air Force Base."

"Oh, great! So you're a North Carolina boy."

"Yes, sir," he replied to Pat. "Not another place in the world have I been stationed that had collards." They all laughed, and he ate another mouthful enthusiastically before adding, "My grandfather on Dad's side was military, and he met my grandmother while serving in Japan. I'm one-fourth Asian," he explained, looking around the table for reactions. The family nodded, smiled, and quietly kept eating.

Hallow leaned toward him. "Will your grandparents be coming to the wedding?"

"Just my grandmother. My grandpa passed away last year." They all mumbled condolences. "Kirsten got to meet him. He thought she was the bee's knees." They giggled.

After finishing her meal, Hallow stood. "Excuse me for a minute. I need to make a quick call." She grabbed her cell phone and walked into the next room, meeting Eve, who also had her phone. They whispered and parted while Kirsten and Will whispered.

Chris came to the table with two pecan pies with whipped cream, followed by Phyllis with a sour cream coconut cake and Pat with a tray of ambrosia—a Holliday family tradition—in wine glasses just as Eve and Hallow sat down again.

They ate desserts with enthusiasm, although most of them were stuffed to discomfort and knew they would be sorry later.

"I have an announcement to make," Hallow said. Everyone turned their attention to her. "Kirsten and Will, I called my colleagues in Raleigh, and none of us have a wedding on Christmas Eve. So, I would like to give you a fabulous wedding and reception in the fellowship hall as my wedding gift to you. I have a small warehouse filled to the brim with amazing items to make that place gorgeous." She grinned.

"Oh, Aunt Hallow! I said small and intimate. No big hullabaloo."

"That would be awesome!" Will said to Hallow with a big smile. "Kirsten deserves the wedding of her dreams. Thank you, Ms...um—"

"It's Aunt Hallow to you, Will."

"And I too, have an announcement," Eve said. "While she was calling Raleigh, I called Mark Stone, the pastor, and he said he'd be delighted to marry you, and the church *is* available."

"Well, this calls for another slice of that pecan pie," Pat spouted and we all laughed.

Jim sat quietly, not feeling at all included in the excitement.

The next three weeks were frenzied as the family worked frantically to get houses and the wedding in place. Kirsten had two showers, had to find a wedding gown, dresses for the mothers and set up a bridal registry with Will. She had no time to go to Rocky Mount, and Eve was relieved since painting still needed to be done on the house she intended to sell. The couple was back and forth between Jacksonville, Atkinson, and

Wilmington while Will's parents and grandmother were visiting friends and family in Goldsboro.

49

December 23

The rehearsal was at the church with only the decorations the church had put up for the holidays. Dinner was catered in the fellowship hall, still a blank slate except for a Christmas tree and the usual tables and chairs. Kirsten's friends set up their instruments in the sanctuary for the next night. Kirsten dressed in a lovely rose-colored dress and Will wore a crew-neck sweater under a black blazer. Jim drove from Rocky Mount to be with Eve, who wore a midnight blue sheath that hugged her body. As the evening progressed, Jim realized that she and the pastor were attracted to each other. Of that there was no doubt.

"Can we talk?" He offered Eve his hand. She followed him down the hall where Sunday School was taught. They stepped into a room.

"Jim? What's going on?"

He ran his fingers through his curls. "Eve, I care about you."

"Oh, well, that's nice, but what's with the secrecy?"

"To be honest, I don't think I should come to the wedding tomorrow."

"Why not?" She looked into his eyes.

"I just don't think it's a good idea. I mean, I don't fit in. I felt very uncomfortable at Thanksgiving and well, I'm even more uncomfortable now."

"I've done all I know to do to let you know I appreciate your help, Jim, but—"

"That's just it. That's *all* there is, Eve. You appreciate my help." His voice owned a sadness she had not heard before. "I care about you. But I don't think you feel the same way."

"Oh!" Eve took a step back. "No, I mean, no, I thank you for all you've done for me, but I don't have any other feelings toward you."

His head drooped.

"I'm sorry, Jim. I didn't know you felt like our relationship could develop into anything more." She touched his hand. Then she looked down the hall toward the fellowship hall. "Look, can we have this conversation some other time? I need to get back to my daughter's dinner."

"I'll walk you back and head on home. I'm not coming to the wedding, but I wish you and Kristen well." He left with a sad look on his face as Eve went back to her seat and Mark Stone sat down beside her.

As planned, Hallow spent the night at the old home place with Chris. Pat and Phyllis would drive back to Wilmington but arrive in time to help decorate the sanctuary the next morning. Eve, Kirsten, Easter, Will and his family would head to Jacksonville.

50

Christmas Eve morning

Hallow and Chris, bundled up in heavy coats with hoods, drove to the front of the church just as four vans from Raleigh pulled up behind them as dawn was breaking. Hallow motioned the drivers toward parking spaces near the back of the church by the fellowship hall. They backed in, got out, and headed in her direction. Easter, Pat, and Phyllis all arrived a few minutes later. They had told Eve she couldn't help so she would be as surprised as Kirsten. She, Kirsten, and Will's mother and grandmother were having manicures, pedicures and hair done in Jacksonville.

"Let's get these front steps done first except for lighting the candles. I'm so relieved that it isn't supposed to rain at all. We can deal with the cold,"

Hallow said, rubbing her arms for warmth. She showed the team her sketch and directed the crew to snug fresh greenery up the ten cement steps and over to the metal rail bases. Once they'd finished, huge clear glass candleholders were nestled in close to the greenery.

"Be gentle with the glass on cement in this cold. They will shatter if you hit them even a tiny bit," Hallow called out. "Know that from experience."

They next added column candles half the size of the others in clear glass. A smaller number of floating candles were included to make the display a little less uniform. When they backed out to the sidewalk to check their progress, they could tell that Hallow was pleased even though she adjusted a few of the glasses.

"I've never seen these front steps look so beautiful," Pat admitted.

"I will have the candles lit forty-five minutes before the wedding begins at 5 pm."

"Won't they burn out?" Easter couldn't imagine them lasting until the wedding was over.

"These are slow-burning candles, Easter. It'll be fine," Hallow explained with a smile. "Wait until you see this lit up tonight. Now let's get up to the vestibule, sanctuary and altar. We have lots to do."

Easter took the elevator up and joined the rest inside the front door.

Two men hauled tall brass candleholders from a van. They placed one on each side of the small vestibule, and a young lady arranged greenery around them.

"I may leave these here or move them down front if we need them. I think with all the trees, we should have enough down there," Hallow said.

The double doors opened and workers came in loaded with boxes and bins. One contained stunning artificial pine boughs with white pearls tucked in the greenery. Another container held yards of white organza. With direction from Hallow, who had moved up to the altar, the team began wrapping the ends of the center aisle pews with the organza before hooking the pine boughs in it.

Easter, who was more of a spectator than a helper, was awed at the ease with which Hallow and her team worked magic. She could never remember this church having such beautiful décor.

"Hey, Hallow, did you miss the part about Kirsten wanting a simple wedding?"

"She didn't say *simple*." She said small and intimate."

"Yeah, with no frills," Chris added with her hands on her hips.

"Well, none of this stuff cost anything! And it's my gift to her," Hallow beamed. "The only things I had to buy were artificial trees that'll be in the fellowship hall."

"Where do you want these live trees, sis?" Pat and another man were coming down the aisle with a large one.

"Get them all up in stands and then I'll place them. There should be seven in all."

"You're putting *seven* Christmas trees on this platform?"

"Yes, Chris. It'll be awesome," Hallow said.

"But where's the pastor going to stand? And the bride and groom?"

"Wide white steps will go below the altar. The pastor will stand just above the steps and Kirsten and Will, on the steps that'll be covered in satin." She turned to Phyllis. "Phyllis, do you have the satin and a staple gun?"

"Yes. As soon as they bring in the steps, I'm on it."

"Great!"

The sisters sat down on the front pew, drank bottles of water, and rested for a few minutes while Pat and the crew got the trees standing up securely. The entire church smelled like a Christmas tree. Two men moved the podium to the choir room and closed the door.

"Oh! What about tree skirts to cover the bases?" Hallow called out. "I didn't think about needing seven or more."

"No problem, Miss Hallow. We brought a box of them. You might want to go through them, though. They're not all white," John Hoke

responded. "I'll get them, and you can decide."
He disappeared as Hallow breathed a sigh of relief.

"Is there going to be a choir?" Easter asked.

"No, just the organ and harp. Kirsten's friends
left them over here last night after the rehearsal.
See? We reserved a place for the harp over here,"
she said, motioning between the organ and the
church's beautiful stained-glass window to where
the beautiful harp had been placed. "I think both
of the musicians went to school with her in Rocky
Mount."

"Oh! I nearly forgot. Girls, don't forget to put
the candles in each of these windows. It'll be
gorgeous at night," she called to her team, who
nodded. Hallow took a couple of deep breaths,
hoping she hadn't forgotten anything else.

"All hands on deck to get these trees sorted
by height." Hallow went to the back of the church
and motioned to each group to move them where
she pointed. When they were in place, the sisters
walked to the back to have a look. Hallow told
the team which trees were to be decorated with
clear lights and which three would have rose-
colored lights.

"Why the rose lights?" Easter's curiosity was
piqued.

"Well, Will is part Asian, so I'm going to try to
do some apple blossoms with the rose lights. If it
doesn't look right, we'll remove the blossoms and

do all white and gold ornaments like the other four trees."

"You already have apple blossoms?"

"My colleague, Tim Sharpe, had some silk ones from an Asian wedding. I figured, what the heck?"

"Here's the box of skirts," John said, plopping the box at Hallow's feet. "I think I saw some pink ones in there." Hallow pilfered through the box and pulled out three pink tree skirts with delight. She also reached for white crocheted skirts to surround the other tree bases. The crew got to work putting lights on the trees.

The trees filled the platform in front of the choir loft to capacity, four trees in clear lights and three with pale rose lights. When they turned them on, everyone in the church gasped.

"I've never seen such a magnificent backdrop for a wedding," Phyllis confessed.

"Breath-taking, sis," Chris said, reaching out to hug Hallow. "Kirsten and Eve will be speechless." Chris couldn't contain her excitement.

"I can't wait to see what it looks like at night with all the candles and trees lit," Easter said with glee.

"Hey!" Mark Stone called from the back of the church. His glasses were off and he ran a hand through his silvering hair. "What have you done to the altar?"

Hallow was undaunted by his outburst. "Oh, come here, pastor. I have to put you in your place."

Mark walked hesitantly to where she was standing with her siblings. "I'm not sure I like the sound of that," he uttered. Easter and Chris giggled at his expression, and he winked at them.

"It's going to be okay. We haven't done any damage, and everything will be returned to its rightful place tomorrow. Come on now." She grabbed him by the hand and hooked her arm through his, pulling him to the front where she placed him above the wide steps, whispering to him as she did.

"It sure does smell good in here," he added.

Chris, Phyllis, Pat, and Easter stood in awe at what their sister had accomplished. She seemed to have it all under control with enough energy to embarrass the Energizer Bunny. But *they* were all tired, especially Chris, who wanted some time to rest before the wedding and reception. Hallow announced they were free to go. Her crew was decorating the reception hall and she'd be around to let the caterers in before she came to the old house on Fourth Street.

"I'll do that, Hallow," Mark told her. "You guys go and rest and dress. I'll let them in if you give me directions on where they set up. I promise to be in a suit when you come back."

"It's already laid out for them, Mark. That would be great."

Pat tapped her arm. "I'll hang out with him, and Phyllis can hang with you ladies, if that's okay.

I'll get my suit and change in the men's bathroom."

"We'll have time to run to my house and change, Pat," Mark said.

"Okay." Phyllis and Pat kissed and she went with Hallow.

Time ticked by as the sisters rested for a few minutes and then worked on their makeup and hair before Kirsten and Eve came through the door with their dresses and shoes in hand. Will's mother, Fe—pronounced Faye—followed close behind with Will's grandmother. The little house was full, and greetings and hugs plentiful. Kirsten and Eve were stunning in their makeup and hair, Kirsten's nails in white and Eve's in a dark berry. Hallow had neither told Easter nor Chris about the wedding gown or the mothers' dresses, so they were delighted when the bags unzipped and revealed the formal attire.

Eve's off-the-shoulder lace dress was floor length with a full skirt that covered her heels, the sleeves extending past her elbow. When Eve slipped it on over her pinned-up hair, her sisters gasped at her beauty. Her shoulders were just tanned enough to show her beautiful skin and rocking body. She decided to wear diamond studs in her ears and no other jewelry.

"You are gorgeous, Eve!" Easter walked over and gave her a big hug. "Jim's mind will be blown when he sees you in this."

"Jim isn't coming," Eve responded. "He said he felt out of place, and to be honest, there's nothing between us other than friendship."

"I'm not sure he feels that way. He was looking at you at Thanksgiving like he was a man in love," Chris said.

"Well, I'm *not*." Eve's voice was emphatic, and she seemed relieved when the bedroom door opened and the conversation ended.

All eyes turned as Will's mother came from the bedroom, dressed in an understated full-length lace shirt-waist dress with a collar and sash that cinched her tiny waist. The color was also red but a shade lighter than Eve's. She, too, had no necklace, and her earrings were diamond studs. She wore her long black straight hair down. Grandmother stepped out in a steel gray lace gown, flats, and a thin silvery topknot with a sprig of apple blossom entwined in it.

"Can y'all help me?" Kirsten stood in the doorway. "I don't want these three ladies to outshine me," she teased.

"That's not going to happen," Eve said.

"Wait, Eve, let me do that," Hallow said, taking her hand.

"No, Hallow. She's *my* daughter and I want to help her into her wedding gown."

"Okay. Call if you need me."

Eve shut the door behind her and heard plenty of giggling from the other side.

"I'm so glad Eve has come to terms with this so quickly," Chris said. They all nodded.

"Who wants champagne?" Easter held up empty flutes. "Courtesy of Pat and Phyllis."

They all turned excitedly to pour some for themselves, Eve, and Kirsten.

"When did y'all ice this down, Phyllis?"

"Pat and I stopped by here before we went to the church and stuck five bottles in the fridge."

"Five bottles?" Easter nearly yelled and then guzzled hers. "I want some more of that."

Laughter filled the small house, and they all turned toward the bedroom door when it opened once again. Eve stuck her head out. "Okay, are you ready to see the most beautiful bride in the whole world?" Eve beamed.

"Yes!"

"Wait! Let me grab my camera. I want lots of pictures for my portfolio," Hallow said, running to get her Canon. The others pulled out cell phones, ready to snap pictures.

"The Holliday paparazzi?" Kirsten's remark brought laughter.

Eve walked behind her daughter and fluffed the short train. They stepped into the living room as everyone stared in awe.

Kirsten's gown had no lace, no bling. Its understated elegance made them all gasp. Kirsten's hair was pulled back in a chignon with a simple satin ribbon. The off-the-shoulder gown with long sleeves fit like a glove, accentuating her small waist, flowing over her hips and cascading into a short, pooled train. Her diamond drop earrings were the only accessory. Even though the gown was plain, it was elegant and timeless. She stepped into white satin heels and Easter handed her some champagne.

"Gosh, I'm already so giddy, I'm afraid to drink it," Kirsten chortled, but she took a sip anyway.

"It's nearly time to go, y'all. Anybody need to use the bathroom before we get in the limo?"Hallow called out.

"What limo?"

"Oh, Kirsten, Pat and I hope you don't mind. We didn't want to pile you into an SUV in that gown. This way we can all ride together," Phyllis announced.

"Thank you so much. Thank all of you for loving me this much." She nearly teared up.

"Don't you dare cry and mess up that makeup," Eve told her.

"Well, let's head to the church!" Kirsten burst out with a big grin. They all clapped and gathered thick shawls or wraps.

"Mama, are you ready to give me away?"

"No. I won't do that, but I will accept Will as my son and his family as my family," Eve said, holding hands with her daughter and smiling at Will's mother and grandmother.

Once in the limo, Hallow instructed the driver to drive the short distance from the house to the church and park in the reserved area right in front. The small town's street lights were dressed in snowflakes as if exclusively for this special occasion. Kirsten and Eve looked out the windows, gasping at the beauty of candlelight all the way up the church steps.

"It's even more beautiful than I could ever have imagined, Aunt Hallow. I'm overwhelmed."

"Well, don't you dare cry and mess up your impeccable makeup!" They all laughed again.

"Are you sure you can climb all those steps in heels, Kirsten?"

"Oh, Mama, I'm walking on air. I'll be fine. I just hope Will is as excited as I am."

"Oh, he is, my dear," Will's mother responded. "Never doubt his love for you."

Hallow, in full wedding planner mode, exited first and told each of them the order of their exit and that they were to stay in the warm limo until she motioned for them. The temperature had dropped ten degrees in the past hour.

Ushers appeared at the top of the steps and the procession began to assemble as Hallow instructed. Ushers escorted Easter and Chris inside to reserved seats near the front. Pat came to greet Phyllis and followed them. Will's father beamed and first escorted his mother into the church, quickly returning to accompany his wife. He didn't come back outside.

"I guess it's our turn, honey."

"I love you, Mama. I hope you can forgive me for taking off when—"

"Not another word about the past. We begin anew today, my darling." Eve kissed her cheek and then wiped away the hint of lipstick she'd left. "Let's not keep Will waiting."

Just inside the vestibule they handed over their wraps to a young lady as the processional began with organ and harp. Eve escorted her daughter down the aisle as the congregation stood and gasped at not only the beautiful bride but also the beautiful mother. Eve glanced at Mark and he blushed, his mouth open in amazement. The wedding was sweet, and Kirsten and Will beamed. They exchanged vows and rings as Mark took every opportunity to glance at Eve, stunned by her beauty.

After the processional, the couple exited the church, gingerly getting down the ten steps with care. They followed the sidewalk to the basement door and went inside, followed by the wedding party. Once there, they waited for the congregation to move from the sanctuary to the fellowship hall with Chris and Easter leading the way. Then the party climbed steep interior steps back to the sanctuary for a photo session, Will and his father helping the ladies reach the top safely.

Meanwhile, Hallow double-checked all the food and instructed Chris and Easter to whisper to folks to find a seat, select tea or coffee beverages, and enjoy light horsd'oeuvres. The long buffet tables were flocked in Christmas red cloths, and the stainless-steel chafing dish handles were each adorned with a red linen napkin. A small lit crystal tree took up little space in the center but offered a lovely glow. Under the lids were boiled shrimp, roast beef, Sashimi, spring rolls, stir fry, General Tso's Chicken, fried chicken, steamed and fried rice, vegetable trays with an array of dips, roasted potatoes, a variety of bread and much more. Two of the room's four corners were decorated with even more Christmas trees of varying sizes.

The 12-layer wedding cake was made of red velvet and chocolate layers and frosted in pure white buttercream that had been sculpted into a winter wonderland. Another smaller cake sat atop it with the same design and edible pine cones spun from sugar and slivered almonds. Further down the table was a smaller groom's cake—a Japanese pagoda to represent Will's Asian heritage. Its sides were dark red with Asian designs and the roof was a beautiful turquoise. Hallow felt certain Will and his family would be delighted.

She ran to the door as Will's family, Eve and Mark Stone entered, the newlyweds following close behind. Kirsten's hand went to her mouth with a look of astonishment and glee.

"Aunt Hallow!" she said, running to hug her aunt, "it's too much. It's just all too much!"

"Never," Hallow said, hugging her back. She then hugged Will who grinned from ear to ear. She escorted them to the reserved table for two while Chris took the rest of the wedding party to their reserved seats.

After the couple fixed their plates and sat down, everybody else feasted on the buffet and chatted. Will's grandmother gave Hallow a thumbs up for the groom's cake and decided to have a slice of both cakes. As the evening passed, Chris couldn't help but notice that Eve and Mark were sitting close and seemed oblivious to their surroundings. She smiled with approval. Mark was a handsome man with a pure heart, and she thought Eve looked happier than she had seen her in many years.

Once the ceremony was over, and the newlyweds and Will's parents had left, Pat, Phyllis, and Easter returned to their homes. Hallow and Chris stayed behind to tidy up before spending one last night at the old house, where they could have separate bedrooms and be closer to Wilmington for Christmas Day. Before leaving the next morning, they planted a FOR SALE sign in the front yard.

51

Christmas Day

The scene could have been a Norman Rockwell poster with Christmas Day at Pat's house. The table was covered with platters of turkey, ham, collards, Dixie Lee peas and relish, rutabagas, corn, rice and gravy, red velvet cheesecake, pecan pie, and ambrosia. Due to the wedding festivities, they had bought most of the food already prepared but it didn't matter. The newlyweds were on their way to Cancun, and places had been set for Pat, Phyllis, Chris, Hallow, Easter, and Eve and an extra place for Jim Townsend or possibly someone else.

When Eve arrived with a beaming Mark Stone instead, the family was not surprised. Hallow and Easter winked at her with approval. Once they were all seated, Pat stood and held up his glass of sweet tea.

"A toast," he announced. "Merry Christmas and Happy New Year to all the Hollidays! And Happy Birthday to Chris." Hallow and Phyllis each touched Chris's arms as Pat continued. "May we *always* remember how blessed we are to be family, and may we all agree to love each other, trust each other, and protect each other, and be happy Hollidays all year 'round."

"Here! Here!" They all chimed in, clinking glasses. Mark said grace, and they feasted.

52: CHRIS

I had often heard the phrase, "You can't go home again." But for the five of us, our last time home changed us, reconnected us, renewed us. We discovered back at the old home place the true value of family and swore an oath to hug and kiss and laugh when we reunited even for a short while and never again to take for granted the importance of love and family.

Family Recipes

Baked Pecans

2 quarts shelled pecan halves
1 stick butter, melted

Preheat oven to 325 degrees. Pour butter over nuts and **turn oven off**. Check after 20 minutes. Salt to taste.

Egg Custard Pie with meringue

4 Tbsp. flour
1 cup sugar
1 tsp vanilla
1 cup milk plus 1 can Carnation milk to make 2 cups
3 eggs, separated
1 pie shell, baked

Preheat oven to 350 degrees. Blend flour and sugar. Slowly whisk in egg yolks. In saucepan, cook on low heat, stirring constantly until thick. Add vanilla and 1 Tbsp. butter. Pour into baked pie shell.

Beat 3 egg whites and add 1/4 tsp. cream of tartar. Gradually beat in 1/4 cup sugar until stiff peaks form. Spread over pie and seal edges. Bake for 15 minutes or until meringue browns.

Mama's Refrigerator Cookies

1 ½ sticks butter, softened
1 cup sugar
1 egg
2 cups self-rising flour
1 cup finely-chopped nuts

Mix together and roll dough into a log. Wrap with Saran and refrigerate until firm.

Slice thinly and bake on ungreased pan in preheated 300-degree oven for about 10 min.

Pepper Relish

12 green peppers, diced
12 red peppers or any combination of colors, diced
10 sweet onions, diced
1 box dark brown sugar
3 Tbl. Salt
1 pint apple cider vinegar

Dice all peppers and onions and add salt. Boil 5 minutes and then simmer for 10 minutes. Drain. Then add sugar and vinegar and boil 5 minutes. Ladle into hot jars and seal.

Daddy's Easy Pickles

1 gal. water
1 cup lime
1 gal. sliced cucumbers

Soak 24 hours. Pour off lime water and rinse well.
To cucumbers, add
3 pts. Apple cider vinegar
6 ¾ cups sugar
2 tsp. pickling spices
2 tsp. salt

Mix and boil until cukes are clear, about 30 minutes.
Ladle into hot jars and seal.

Pear Preserves

8 cups sliced pears
3 cups sugar
1 cup water
Lemon slices

Boil sugar and water for 5 minutes. Add pears and
lemon slices and boil until thickened and tender (about 3
hours) on low heat. Watch. Don't let syrup burn!

Never Fail Fudge

5 cups sugar
1 tall can evaporated milk
2 sticks butter
3 12 oz. bags chocolate chips
1 tsp. vanilla

Boil first 3 ingredients for 6 minutes. Pour over rest of ingredients. Beat until smooth. Add nuts if desired. Spread into buttered broiler pan. Let stand 3-6 hours. (You can refrigerate and cut in less time.) Cut into squares. Makes about 5 pounds!

Ambrosia

Oranges, 10-12, peeled and pith removed
Sugar, ½ cup or sweeter to taste
Pecans, ½ cup, chopped
Coconut,1 cup of Bird's Eye, thawed (not Baker's!)

Combine all ingredients except pecans a day ahead. Refrigerate. Add nuts an hour before serving with whipped cream. Cherry on top is optional.

Lemon Meringue Pie

1 can Equal Brand condensed milk
½ cup lemon juice
1 tsp. lemon zest
3 eggs, separated into yolks and whites
1 graham cracker crust
¼ tsp. cream of tartar
¼ cup sugar

In medium bowl mix together milk, lemon juice and zest. Blend in 3 egg yolks. Pour into crust and set aside. Preheat oven to 325 degrees.

Beat egg whites and add cream of tartar. Gradually beat in sugar until stiff peaks form. Spread over pie and seal edges. Bake 12-15 minutes until meringue browns.

Reviews For Susan's Books

Genesis Beach

"…a spine-tingling mystery…Add the Logan Hunter series to your reading list." Lynette Hall Hampton, *Echoes of Mercy*

"…engaging characters, a tight plot and a beautiful, yet unpredictable setting. Pack this one for the beach and enjoy the first book in a promising series." Mary Fran Vesey, *Murder at Treese Family Inn*

"…holds your interest to the very end." Martha Cheves, *Stir, Laugh, Repeat*

"Whitfield crafted an enjoyable mystery filled with vibrant character, capturing the essence of coastal North Carolina." K.R. Jones, *The Ghosts of Guantanamo Bay*

Just North of Luck

"Whitfield takes the reader to the backwoods of North Carolina…[and] weaves a tale that leaves us breathless…" Sylvia Dickey Smith, *Dance on His Grave* and *Deadly Sins-Deadly Secrets*

"…eloquent descriptions of the Blue Ridge Mountains and grisly murders that take place in that beautiful setting will haunt readers." Sunny Frazier, *Fools Rush In*

"Not for the faint of heart." Mark Stevens, *Antler Dust*

"Just North of Luck grabs you by the scruff of the neck and takes you on a harrowing ride from the very beginning... The second book in the Logan Hunter series is a must read." Elise Crawford, *A Promise Kept*

"Quirky characters, humor, and a keen sense of place..." Bob Avery, *Beneath A Buried House*

"Just south of sanity!" Apex Reviews

Hell Swamp

"...a Carolina Low Country tale of greed and misguided deeds. Fasten your seat belt!" Maggie Bishop, *Murder at Blue Falls*

"...Hell Swamp is a good old-fashioned roller coaster ride. Whitfield sprinkles in humorous and colorful descriptions...enough for an occasional chuckle in a tense situation." David Fingerman, *Silent Kill*

"Hell Swamp...riveting from page one, you'll want to read with all the lights on and the doors locked." Teresa Jenner Garrido, *Wind Whisperer*

"The action in Hell Swamp jumps out at you from the first chapter and never lets up. Edgy stuff." Mary Deal, *River Bones*

"...well-written, suspenseful mystery with a likeable protagonist, vivid imagery, a taste of horror, a little tongue-in-cheek humor and even romance. What's not to like?" All Books Review

"Whitfield has drawn a cast of characters from down by the Black River…peculiar, scary and injected with just enough humor to make Hell Swamp stand out from the pack. Read the book. It's a good 'un." Tom Cooke, *Memoirs of Bear*

Killer Recipes

"Don't be afraid to try these concoctions. We only write about murder and poison, we don't participate in them." J.D. Webb, *Smudge*

"Titles are hilarious…recipes are real and delicious. Whitfield has put a fun slant on the old standard cookbook." Mary Deal, *Down To The Needle*

"I'm giving copies to friends for gifts…a worthwhile addition to my cookbook collection." Gayle Wigglesworth, *Mud To Ashes*

Sin Creek

"This action-packed mystery will keep you turning the pages until its shocking end." L.J. Sellers, *The Sex Club* and *Secrets To Die For*

"Lickety-split pace and effective description [in Sin Creek] give the reader the feeling that they are conducting the investigation right along with Logan Hunter. If you're a fan of mysteries, this one is guaranteed not to disappoint. If mystery's not your usual genre, make an exception with Sin Creek. Like the Cyclone at Coney Island, Sin Creek is gripping and intense, yet an enjoyable ride." Mark Rosendorf, *The Rasner Effect*

Slightly Cracked

"...a tale of friendship served with a dollop of humor."
Laurel-Rain Snow, *Vine Voice*

"Humor and pathos. Lifelong friendship and devotion."
Jacqueline Seewald, *Blood Family*

Sprig of Broom

"A useful and interesting insight into a confusing period of history often referred to as 'When God and His angels slept.'" Carol Peak, Amazon Review

"Walk the royal castle halls, smell the stench of common places, cross the English Channel, and observe a proud father as he swaddles his offspring with no knowledge of how history will depict the Plantagenet Kings of England." Cold Coffee Press

About Author Susan Whitfield

Award-winning multi-genre author Susan Whitfield is a native of North Carolina, where she sets all of her novels. She is the author of five published mysteries, *Genesis Beach, Just North of Luck, Hell Swamp, Sin Creek and Sticking Point*. She also authored *Killer Recipes*, a unique cookbook that includes recipes from mystery writers around the country. *Slightly Cracked* is her first women's fiction, set in Wayne County where she lives with her husband. *Sprig of Broom* is her first historical fiction. Their two sons live nearby with their families.

Susan's a member of Mystery Writers of America, Sisters in Crime, Coastal Carolina Mystery Writers, and North Carolina Writers Network. Her books are available in print and ebook formats. Susan is currently researching a medieval ancestor for an historical mystery.